P9-DFO-426

DISCARDED

GAME ON

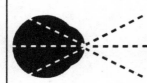

This Large Print Book carries the
Seal of Approval of N.A.V.H.

GAME ON

LILLIAN DUNCAN

THORNDIKE PRESS
A part of Gale, Cengage Learning

GALE
CENGAGE Learning·

Farmington Hills, Mich • San Francisco • New York • Waterville, Maine
Meriden, Conn • Mason, Ohio • Chicago

GALE
CENGAGE Learning®

Copyright © 2016 by Lillian Duncan.
Thorndike Press, a part of Gale, Cengage Learning.

ALL RIGHTS RESERVED
This is a work of fiction. Names, characters, places, and incidents either are the product of the author's imagination or used fictitiously and any resemblance to actual persons, living or dead, business establishments, events, or locales is entirely coincidental.

Thorndike Press® Large Print Christian Mystery.
The text of this Large Print edition is unabridged.
Other aspects of the book may vary from the original edition.
Set in 16 pt. Plantin.

LIBRARY OF CONGRESS CATALOGING-IN-PUBLICATION DATA

Names: Duncan, Lillian (Novelist), author.
Title: Game on / by Lillian Duncan.
Description: Large print edition. | Waterville, Maine : Thorndike Press, 2017. |
    Series: Thorndike Press large print christian mystery
Identifiers: LCCN 2017015636| ISBN 9781432841089 (hardcover) | ISBN 1432841084
    (hardcover)
Subjects: LCSH: Women private investigators—Fiction. | Legislators—United
    States—Fiction. | Stalking—Fiction. | Christian fiction. | Mystery fiction. | Large
    type books.
Classification: LCC PS3604.U5286 G36 2017 | DDC 813/.6—dc23
LC record available at https://lccn.loc.gov/2017015636

Published in 2017 by arrangement with Pelican Ventures, LLC

Printed in Mexico
1 2 3 4 5 6 7 21 20 19 18 17

This and all I do is for God's glory. As always to my amazing husband — my partner in life and in writing! To the wonderful doctors and nurses who've taken such good care of me since being diagnosed with brain tumors and NF 2, especially Dr. Steven Rosenfeld and Erin Vogan — because of your compassionate and excellent care, I can still hear the words I love to write!

1

Lucas McMann walked down the street, pretending everything was normal. With his premature gray hair and his expensive suit, he looked the part of a senator even if he wasn't one yet. And he never would be — if something didn't change soon.

Scanning the area, his heart rate increased with every step. Only the strictest discipline kept him from breaking into a run. If he did that, then they'd know he knew.

He didn't know why he'd been chosen to play the game. He didn't know what they wanted. He didn't even know who they were. There were many things he didn't know about the game, but Lucas knew one thing. In the end, he would be the winner.

The situation was intolerable, possibly even dangerous.

As he forced his footsteps to slow, his gaze flitted from person to person. Was the young girl with spiked pink hair one of them? Or the older man dressed as a tourist? Or the well-dressed man pretending to be a businessman?

It could be any of them or all of them. They were everywhere. No matter where he went, he couldn't get away from their prying eyes or their cameras. And now not even his home was safe. As they'd proven last week.

The Washington Monument towered over the city.

After all that he'd lost, his career was the only thing he had left. He'd never become the next US senator from North Carolina if he couldn't stop them. There was no way he could focus on the upcoming election if these people kept hounding him.

It was part of the plan his father had mapped out years before. It had worked perfectly up to this point. First, local government, then the state. He'd been a US congressman for the past four years. Now it was time to move up to the Senate. Each step moved him closer to his ultimate goal — the White House.

President Lucas McMann? He wasn't even sure how he felt about that anymore. But his father had wanted this so badly, Lucas owed it to his dad to at least try now that he'd passed.

Focusing on the well-known landmark, Lucas regained a little more control of his thoughts, his emotions, and his rationality.

To win this game, he needed a new plan — one to stop them.

To end the game for good.

Lucas approached a café. The sidewalk was filled with tourists and residents enjoying springtime in DC after a harsh winter. He bypassed the only empty table and went inside. He chose a seat facing the door. His muscles relaxed.

A waiter came up. "Know what you want"

"A black coffee and a croissant."

"Be right back."

Lucas stared at the door.

A man walked in with a camera and aimed it at him.

Lucas grabbed a menu to put it in front of his face but was too late.

The man gave a wave and walked out with a satisfied grin.

The waiter brought his order.

Lucas gritted his teeth. For weeks, he'd been reacting to them, but no more. It was time for him to step up to the plate and make a game-changing play. It wouldn't be easy since he didn't know the rules, the players, or even the goal. He would have to step out of the box. Do the unexpected so he could take control. Then he would end it.

The waiter stopped at his table. "Need anything else?"

Lucas glanced at his name tag. "Thanks, Nick, I'm fine."

Lucas fixated on the man's name. Nick. The name conjured up a glimmer of an idea. A person who might be able to help. Could she be the answer?

Lucas paid the bill and walked out. He stopped and blinked several times as if the sunshine was too bright. In reality, he was searching for them. Nobody seemed to be paying attention to him. He sauntered back towards the Capitol Building. Almost time for his appointment.

The plan was for the current senator to announce his retirement tomorrow and throw his support to Lucas. At the same time, Lucas would officially announce his bid for the Senate. Even though he'd unofficially been a candidate for the better part of a year.

A twenty-something woman walked towards him, a camera slung around her neck. She met his gaze and smiled. Actually, more of a smirk. Her hand caressed the camera slung around her neck. Another one.

His pulse rate skyrocketed.

Not waiting for the crosswalk, he zig-zagged his way through stopped cars. Once he'd made it to the other side, he half-jogged, half-walked down the block.

"Mr. McMann," a young voice called. "Mr. McMann."

He slowed down and turned.

A young boy about eight or nine stood with a camera and a hopeful look. "Can I get a picture of you?"

Was he part of the game? It didn't seem likely. Taking a deep breath, Lucas smiled. "Sure thing, buddy."

His father walked over. "I told him you'll probably be the next senator from North Carolina. But I didn't mean for him to bother you."

Lucas smiled. "He's not a bother."

The boy snapped a few pictures. "Thanks, Senator McMann."

"I'm not a senator yet, son. But it does have a nice ring to it." Lucas laughed even as he searched for the woman. She stood on the other side of the street, watching. Woman or not, he wouldn't ruin this boy's day in his nation's capital. "Hey, how about a selfie with the two of us?"

Grinning, the boy ran his hand through his hair as if that could improve his curly brown mop.

Lucas slung an arm around his shoulder while the boy held the phone camera at arm's length. When he was finished, he said, "Wow. My teacher will be impressed."

"Maybe you'll get some extra credit."

The woman across the street lifted her camera.

He turned his back and focused on the boy. "Where are you from?"

"We're from Wade, North Carolina." The boy's grin revealed a missing tooth. "Just like you. It's a really small town."

"My hometown of Maiden is small too."

The boy's father shook Lucas's hand. "Nice of you to take time for my son. It's our first visit here."

"It's a beautiful city." Lucas glanced back at the woman. "Let me call my assistant and tell her to give you the VIP tour of the Capitol and the White House. What's your name?" After scheduling the VIP tour, Lucas said his goodbyes.

Anger coursed through him. Time to make that game-changing play. He sprinted down the street. Just before he turned the corner, he glanced back. She was still there, running to catch up.

Game on, lady! Let's see who can run faster.

People he passed looked alarmed, but he ignored them. He scanned the crowd. After

12

several deep breaths, he smiled in triumph.

The woman was nowhere to be seen.

Now was the time to gain the advantage. He needed help. Someone he could trust. Someone with investigative experience. Someone those people wouldn't know. His mind flashed back to the waiter's name tag.

If she'd talk to him.

If she'd help him.

If she'd forgotten all about the past.

But those were mighty big ifs.

2

Nikki Kent gritted her teeth as she made a U-turn. What a way to start the day. Well, not exactly the start — it was almost noon. But as a private investigator, her days weren't nine to five. They might start at noon, like today, or at midnight.

On the track of a philandering husband, and she'd forgotten her camera. Oh well, it wouldn't take but a minute to pick up her camera at the office and get back to the seedy motel. They'd still be there, no doubt.

Nikki pulled into the strip mall where her office was located.

A man stood in front of the window that proudly announced this was the home of Kent Investigations. A new client perhaps?

Putting on her professional smile, she stepped out of her car.

He turned towards her.

Their gazes met.

An angry spark ignited inside Nikki. In an

instant, the spark grew into a bonfire.

Lucas McMann walked towards her with a smile, his arms moving into position as if to hug her. "Nikki. You look beautiful."

She sidestepped his outstretched arms. "What are you doing here"

"Sorry about dropping in on you out of the blue, but I figured if I called, you'd hang up." His voice had that slow Southern drawl she remembered, like warm honey.

Her heart thumped. She told herself it was only from the shock of him showing up unannounced. Of course, he was right. She would have hung up on him in a heartbeat, then had her phone disconnected. And maybe moved out of the area for good measure. But she wouldn't admit it. "You don't know what I would do or not do."

"Why don't we go inside so we can talk in private?"

"We have nothing to talk about, and I'm in a hurry. I only stopped here to pick up something."

Lucas put a hand on her arm. "Don't be that way, Nikki. I know things ended badly with us, but that was years ago. I need your help."

Ended badly? That was an understatement.

"Need my help?" Her laugh was bitter as

she removed his hand from her arm. He hadn't come here to give her a way-overdue apology, but because he needed something. Typical of the Mighty McManns. "That is priceless, but I don't think so."

"You can't turn me down without at least hearing what I have to say."

Two customers from another store gawked at them. She didn't need a scene, so she marched to her office door and unlocked it. She turned to Lucas. "In fact, I can do just that." Nikki opened the door, and then closed it before he could come in. She smiled at him as she turned the lock.

His look of shock was genuine. He knocked.

"Go away, Lucas."

He knocked louder. "I'm not leaving until you talk to me."

She shook her head. How could she get out of here? She could use the back door, but her car was out front. Certainly he'd notice her walking to the car.

After a moment, he fished out his cell phone and hit some numbers.

Her phone rang.

Lucas smiled and pointed to the phone number on the door.

Acting this way was beneath the new Nikki. Sometimes it was so hard to be a

Christian. She unlocked the door.

Lucas sauntered in, still smiling. Didn't anything ruffle those political feathers of his? "Shall we try this again? Good afternoon, Nikki."

"It was until a few minutes ago, Lucas. Or should I call you Senator? Which do you prefer?"

"I'm not a senator yet. And even if I were, you could still call me Lucas."

"Actually, I don't plan to call you anything." She placed her hands in her lap to keep them from shaking. She forced her voice to sound calm and reasonable. "I don't have time for this. You need to leave. I really do have things to do. Some of us have to work for a living."

"I want to hire you."

How could he even think she'd consider such a thing? "I choose whom I work for and whom I do not work for. You can be sure I won't work for you. Not now, not ever."

She looked at the yellow sticky note attached to her computer monitor. *FORGIVE-NESS* was written in huge capital letters. It was her God word of the month. She'd made a commitment to not only study the fruits of the Spirit, but to cultivate them in her everyday life. Her Christian mentor had

17

assured her she could do it. That nothing was too difficult when one put God in control of one's life. Her fingernails tapped on her desk. *Jesus said to forgive our enemies.*

Lucas might not be her enemy, but he was close.

But this . . . this was much more than she'd bargained for. Never in a million years had she thought she'd ever come face to face with Lucas McMann again.

This wasn't a test she'd expected, nor could she pass it. She opened the drawer and picked up the camera. "Lucas, I don't have time for this. I am in hot pursuit of a philandering husband. He just gave me the perfect opportunity to prove it to my client — his wife."

"Can't it wait?"

"No. As I said, some of us have to work for a living."

He flinched as if she'd slapped him. She brushed away the momentary guilt. Surely he hadn't thought she'd welcome him with a smile and a hug.

"I don't blame you for being angry." His voice was calm and rational, just the opposite of what she was feeling. "But it was years —"

"Don't flatter yourself. That was years

18

ago." She'd thought she was over it until now.

"I'll pay you whatever you want."

"You think your money can buy me." Her voice was tinged with rage. "But I'm not for sale. I am not my parents."

"That's not what I meant, Nikki. Give me a break here. I'm in trouble, and you're the only one I trust." He sounded sincere, but that meant nothing.

"That doesn't speak well for you or your friends, does it?"

"I guess it doesn't." He grinned. "I'm only asking for a few minutes of your time. I know I have no right to ask anything of you, but please listen to me."

"Sorry, I really don't have the time." She gravitated towards the door.

"Fine, give me a time and I'll meet you back here later."

Instead of answering him, she opened the door and motioned for him to leave.

He sighed but walked out.

After locking the door, Nikki turned to him. "One of the good things about owning my own business is there's no one to tell me what to do. Hire someone else. I can give you a list of some good investigators."

"I want you."

Her heart cracked just a little. He'd told

her that once before. She walked to her car.

He followed. "I think you'd change your mind if you'd only listen to me."

Her response was to hit the unlock button on her car. "Sorry, Lucas. The McManns can't always get their way." As she slid into her seat, another sticky note on the dashboard caught her eye. *PATIENCE.* To remind her to be nicer when she drove.

The passenger door opened. Lucas slid in just as the car started moving.

"Lucas, get out of my car. I don't have time for this."

"This really is important. I'm not leaving until I talk to you."

"Get out of my car." Her gaze moved up to the sticky note. She added, "Please."

"Go follow that philandering husband. I'll sit here quietly until you have the time to talk with me. Better hurry before he leaves."

Why wouldn't he leave her alone?

She really did need to get to that motel.

Instead of answering him, she put the car in gear and then turned the radio up full blast. Even if he tried to talk, she wouldn't be able to hear him. She refused to give in to the twinge of curiosity. He had no right to ask anything of her. Anger surged through her once again.

A moment later, he joined in with the

song. Lucas knew the words to a Christian praise song? Surprising.

Her heart thumped as his deep, rich baritone filled every space of her car. How was she supposed to ignore him? Her hands tightened on the steering wheel as she gritted her teeth, determined to not let him get to her. *Focus on the traffic, not Lucas or that beautiful voice.*

Why was the one person she would never forgive sitting beside her? *Certainly You don't want me to forgive him, do You, Lord? He doesn't deserve it.* In her heart, she knew God's answer. She hadn't deserved forgiveness either, but God had gladly given it to her.

When Nikki got to the motel, she grabbed her camera and finally looked at Lucas. "Stay in the car. Or I'll take your picture at this no-tell motel and post it all over the web. I'm sure your opponents would love that."

"Whatever you say. Your wish is my command."

That charming little grin of his that she'd once loved so much only managed to irritate her. That proved she was over him. "If that were true, you wouldn't be sitting in my car."

"I just want you to listen. But we can talk

about all that later." He motioned for her to go. "Take care of your business. I don't want to interfere with you making a living."

"Promise me that you'll stay in the car. No matter what."

"Whatever you say."

"That wasn't really a promise." But it would have to do. She grabbed the camera and marched towards room seven, hoping she wasn't too late.

The happy couple stepped out of the room arm in arm.

Nikki lifted her camera and clicked five photos in quick succession with the cheap motel sign flashing in the background. She'd earned her money this time.

"Hey, what are you doing?" the man yelled out at her.

Time to go. Nikki lowered her camera as she turned towards her car. Now his wife could get the alimony she deserved.

"Hey, I'm talking to you."

Nikki quickened her steps. A hand grabbed her shoulder and twirled her around.

"I said, what are you doing?" His mottled-red face was an angry mask.

"Back off." She stepped back with her hands in a surrender position, the camera hung around her neck. "I don't want any trouble. I'm leaving."

"Not before you give me that camera." He stepped towards her.

"That's not going to happen."

"Give me that camera." He made a grab for it.

"Stop it!" Nikki jumped back.

"Give her some money, Stanley." The woman stepped up and looped her arm through his. "Just pay her more than your money-grubbing wife, and she'll give you the pictures. That's how those people are."

"Good idea, Macy." He beamed at the woman and then turned back to Nikki. "How much will it take for you to give me those pictures instead of my wife?"

"Sorry, they aren't for sale."

"Then I want that camera." He lunged at her. "Give it to me. I mean it."

Nikki pushed him away with her free hand.

Stanley stumbled but charged at her again, his face red and angry.

Macy came at Nikki from the side and pushed her off balance.

Nikki shoved her away with ease, but that gave Stanley time to grab the camera. The strap tightened around her neck as he pulled on it. "Stop it."

His response was to tug even harder.

OK, she'd tried reasonable — it hadn't worked. Nikki moved in close and elbowed him in the stomach. His hold loosened. Nikki pulled the camera from his grasp.

Lucas had an enraged expression on his face as he opened the car door.

"Stay in the car. I can handle this."

Stanley grabbed the camera. "You aren't going to ruin my life." He glared as he twisted her wrist.

Instead of answering, she moved forward to relieve the pressure around her neck.

Macy jumped at her from behind, grabbing her hair.

That was it!

Now she was mad. In one fluid motion, Nikki let go of Stanley, then bent low so the strap slipped from around her neck. He could keep the stupid thing. She could always take more pictures. The man probably wouldn't even end his affair after all this.

Nikki turned towards Macy and flipped her onto the ground.

Stanley held the trophy — her camera. "Hey, don't you hurt her," he yelled.

"Then give me back my camera." She moved forward.

"No way." He tucked the camera into his arm as if it were a football.

"Last chance. Give my camera back. You don't want to get arrested, do you?"

"Me? You're the one who needs to be arrested."

"It's not against the law to take pictures."

3

Wow. Nikki really could take care of herself.

Lucas had to fight the urge to help. That probably wouldn't make her agree to work for him though. He'd hoped she'd be over their mangled teenage romance, but that didn't seem to be the case. Promise or not, if it looked as if she was in danger, he wouldn't sit there and do nothing.

A police car with flashing lights pulled in. Good. The cavalry had arrived.

As the officer stepped out of his car, Lucas did the same.

The officer moved towards Nikki and the couple. "Break it up." The officer turned to the man. "Back up a few steps, sir."

"I'm not the one causing the problem. It's her." The businessman pointed at Nikki, then at the woman who was still on the ground. "She assaulted my friend. Arrest her."

The officer glared at Nikki.

"He stole my camera." Nikki spoke in a calm voice. She must be used to this type of situation. "And she attacked me first. Pulled my hair."

The officer walked over to the woman on the ground, his gaze clearly on her thigh. Her tight red dress had moved up several inches during the wrestling match. He helped her up. "Are you all right, miss?"

"I suppose, but . . ."

"What's going on here?"

Macy launched into a tirade.

Nikki stared hard at Lucas and then shook her head. Why wouldn't she let him help?

"Look, I can explain, Officer," Nikki said. "If you would just listen to me."

"I'll get to you when I get to you." He turned back to Macy, who was making quite the show of brushing herself off. "Are you sure you're all right, miss?"

"I guess so. She knocked me on the ground." The woman pouted, but then gave Nikki a smug look as if to say, *I win.*

Lucas had heard enough. He wouldn't let Nikki get in trouble when she hadn't been at fault. She'd just have to be angry that he interfered.

Another cruiser pulled in as the officer turned to Nikki. Lucas decided to wait another moment to see what would happen next.

"She attacked me first." Nikki's tone was reasonable.

"I'll let you know when I want you to talk." The officer glared.

As the other officer stepped out of his cruiser, Nikki smiled. The man winked at Nikki as he walked up. "What's going on, Sam?"

"Apparently, this woman assaulted these people, Rob."

"Really. That doesn't sound much like Ms. Kent."

"You know her?"

"She used to be on the force. Now she's a law-abiding private investigator serving the fine people of Jacksonville. I doubt very much if she assaulted anyone unless she was attacked first."

"Oh." The younger officer's face turned slightly pink. "I didn't know."

"If you don't mind, I'll handle this," Rob said.

"No problem." The first officer walked back to his cruiser.

Macy didn't look quite as smug

Rob turned to Nikki. "What's happening?"

"He stole my camera and attacked me." Nikki pointed at the businessman. "Then she jumped on my back."

"That belong to her?" Rob asked Stanley.

The man nodded.

"Then I guess you should give it back to her, don't you think?"

"But she took pictures of me. She had no right to do that. Make her erase them."

"There's nothing illegal about her taking pictures."

Lucas grimaced. Unfortunately, the officer was right. It wasn't against the law to take someone's picture, especially a public figure like himself. But did that mean people had the right to stalk him? Maybe he shouldn't have come to Nikki. She made a living taking pictures of people who didn't want them taken. Nikki might not see anything wrong with what was happening.

The officer took the camera and handed it back to Nikki.

"She attacked my girlfriend."

"I defended myself," Nikki said, her tone calm.

The girlfriend pointed at Nikki. "This is all her fault. She had no —"

"I'm sorry you got caught having a little fling with your boss. But you had no right to attack me," Nikki interjected.

"We offered her money," the man grumbled.

The officer cracked a smile. "That probably didn't go well. Ms. Kent, you have the right to press charges. If you want to."

"Are you kidding me?" Stanley sounded astonished.

"I warned you." Nikki smiled. "I'll give you a break. Besides, after your wife gets through with you, you probably wouldn't be able to afford the fine anyway." She pointed at the girlfriend. "And he sure won't be able to afford you."

The blonde held her head up proudly. "I'll have you know I love Stanley. Not his money."

"Good thing. Since Stanley won't have nearly as much after the divorce."

"OK, you two are free to go." Rob nodded at the couple. "Next time you don't like something someone's doing, walk away."

Stanley nodded at the officer and then glared at Nikki. "You don't think it'll make any difference, do you? My wife will forgive me. She always does." Stanley stomped off with Macy hurrying behind.

Lucas now had no doubt Nikki was the one who could help him — if only he could talk her into it.

Nikki moved towards Robbie's cruiser. "Thanks, Robbie."

"Not a problem." He followed her. "You're looking good these days, Kent. I haven't seen you around in a while. Where've you been hiding yourself?"

"Been busy, and I've given up the bar scene." She lowered her voice, not wanting Lucas to hear their conversation. Her life was none of his business.

"Hey, I heard you broke up with Don. You ready to finally take your chances with me?" He leaned against the hood of his cruiser.

"Sorry, Robbie. No relationships — at least not for a long time. It's time for me to get my act together."

"Oh, come on, Nikki. But I see you've already found a new vict— I mean, guy." He laughed.

"Very funny."

"The problem is you haven't found the right guy." He grinned. "You never know, he might be right here in this parking lot with you and you don't realize it."

"Very subtle, Rob."

"I thought so. Give me a jingle if you change your mind. And stop getting into fights."

"It wasn't my fault." Nikki opened his door for him.

He slid into the driver's seat. "Be good and be safe, Nikki."

31

"You do the same, Robbie. I only deal with cheating husbands who don't want to get caught. You're the one who deals with the real criminals."

"That's for sure. See you around, Nikki." He held his hand up to his ear. "Call me."

She laughed and then got into her own car. "You're still here."

"I told you I wasn't leaving until you listen to me. But let me say that was quite impressive. It made me even more determined to hire you." Lucas grinned at her.

"It's part of the job."

"I can't believe you managed to handle them. I wanted to help. But since you told me to stay in the car, I did."

"You didn't exactly stay in the car."

"I wanted to be ready in case. I can see I came to the right person for help." He smiled that charming smile. "Are you ready to listen now?"

In answer to his question, she leaned over and turned the radio on, but not quite as loud as before. "I need to decompress."

"I can understand that. You and that officer seemed very chummy."

"Really?"

"Sorry, just an observation. Decompress away." He turned the radio up another notch and sang along.

Was Stanley right? Would his wife really forgive him? Nikki didn't have that much forgiveness in her. Which was exactly why she wasn't married anymore. Forgiving someone always seemed like giving them permission to do it again. But the Bible was clear. Forgiving others was part of being a Christian. She probably could learn to forgive for the little things. But the big things? That was a whole different story. She'd need God's help for that. She gave a sideways glance at her passenger. Forgiving him didn't seem possible. But then again . . . *with God all things are possible.*

Back at her office, she shut off the car and looked at Lucas. "I appreciate that you came all this way, but politics are not my thing. I am not the right person to help you." As if that was the reason she was refusing. Not the fact that he'd broken her heart and ruined her life.

To be fair, she'd done her own share of ruining with one failed marriage, but still . . .

"This isn't about politics. It's about me." He stared at her with those pale blue eyes.

"Oh, please. If it's about you, it's about politics." She heard the bitterness in her voice and didn't like it. She left Lucas sitting in her car and went into her office.

When she sat down at her desk, the sticky note caught her gaze once more. *I can't do this, God. I really can't.*

The bell above her door tinkled.

"Are you ready to listen now?" Lucas was persistent, probably one of the characteristics that made him a good politician.

She glared at him. "Why would I do that?"

"I could say because we cared about each other once, but I don't think you're in the mood to hear that. So how about because you love this country?"

"Excuse me?"

"You couldn't even sing the national anthem all the way through without crying."

Her face warmed. She couldn't believe he remembered anything about her, let alone that. "And what does that have to do with you?"

"I'm not saying what's happening to me is a threat to national security, but there is a possibility that it could be. After all, I am a US congressman and might be a senator soon."

"Appealing to my patriotism?" She had to give him credit. "You're pulling out all the stops, aren't you?"

He grinned at her. "I wouldn't say that."

"I would." Out of the corner of her eye,

she saw the yellow sticky note. She was beginning to hate that word. "If I listen, will you go away?"

He nodded.

"OK, I'll listen. Then I'll tell you no."

"Way to keep an open mind, Nikki." He grinned as he sat down. "Can we talk about — ?"

"No, we can't." He hadn't cared for the past sixteen years, and he didn't care now. But he needed something from her, so he was willing to pretend if it meant she would be more agreeable. "Do you want to tell me what your problem is or not? I've got other things to do today."

"Better yet, I can show you. If you look me up on social media, you'll see what I'm talking about."

She typed in the address he dictated.

Nikki wasn't the insecure teenaged girl he'd known. She was a beautiful and confident woman who wasn't afraid to tell him what she thought. She didn't seem to be the least bit intimidated by the fact he might become a US senator.

Two of her best qualities had been her sweetness and her honesty. She was still honest, but he wasn't so sure about sweetness after the scene he'd just witnessed. No one bullied her these days. He didn't think even his father would have the nerve. If his father could see Nikki now, he'd be impressed with the woman she'd become.

It was hard to believe sixteen years had passed since the last time Lucas had stared into those emerald-green eyes. He'd come here on the assumption she was over their past. That didn't seem to be the case. Not that he blamed her. Nikki had every right not to help him, but he hoped to change her mind. He prayed for the right words to convince her.

Nikki's expression went from anger to curiosity to concern as she stared at the monitor.

He didn't have to look to know what she was seeing. His page was filled with pictures of himself in all sorts of situations and places. The pictures were accompanied by captions that said things like *I see you* or *I'm watching you* or something similar.

"OK, this is a bit creepy. I'll give you that." She looked up at him. "So, what is this about?"

"I appear to be part of some sort of internet game."

"A game?"

"I know it sounds odd and it's hard to explain, but it's some weird version of hide-

36

and-seek. And apparently, I'm it. I can't get away from them. Everywhere I go, they are there taking pictures of me."

"And" — she held up both hands — "you're a politician. A public figure. People like to take your picture. So what?"

"Like I said, it's hard to explain. They aren't regular picture takers. Just today one of them chased me down the streets of DC. I was determined not to let her get my picture, and I won the game. At least for today."

Confusion crossed her face, then doubt. "You came all the way to Florida to see me because of some game. I don't think so."

"I know it sounds bizarre."

"It doesn't sound bizarre — it sounds as if you're making the whole thing up. You're a public figure — people have a right to take your picture."

Why couldn't he make people understand? "True, but they don't have the right to stalk me, do they?"

"Excuse me for not believing you. Why don't you tell me the real reason you're here?"

He had to make her understand how much he needed her help finding these people. "I'm not lying, Nikki. Everywhere I go, people are stalking me. Following me.

Taking pictures of me. More than the usual 'Oh, look, there's Congressman McMann. Let's get a picture.' I need someone I can trust to find out who they are and why they're doing it. So I can make them stop. I need you to believe me."

Her expression softened for a moment. But her voice was cold when she asked, "Believe you? Why? Because you've been so trustworthy in the past."

Her words were sharp, but he couldn't argue the truth in them. He'd once told her that he loved her and then walked away. Because it was the easy thing to do. Because it's what his father wanted. But that was years ago — a lifetime ago. He'd hoped Nikki wouldn't still be angry. Apparently, she was. Even so, he wasn't ready to give up yet. "Nikki, I know how much I hurt you. I am so —"

"I don't need your apology. Even though I'm sure it would be wonderful, I'm all grown up now. I know pretty words aren't the same as the truth." Her tone was harsh and cynical.

Had he been the one to make that happen? He probably wasn't the only one — but there was no doubt he'd been the first one. The Nikki he knew was so sweet, so kind to everyone. He met her gaze head-on.

"I've never lied to you, Nikki. Not once."

She bit her lip but said nothing. Tears misted her eyes. The first glimpse of the Nikki he'd known.

He forged ahead. "It started out with pictures, and that wasn't too bad. But now they've moved on from pictures and are messing with my phones and computers." He hurried on before she could kick him out. "Sometimes when I try to call someone, the number has vanished. Or an email address that I've used dozens of times will suddenly be gone."

"Computers aren't always the most reliable. Things like that happen."

"Then last week, they started having things delivered to me that I didn't order."

"What kind of things?"

"Books. DVDs and even pizzas from my local pizzeria."

"Maybe you forgot you ordered them."

"I didn't forget that I ordered twenty-five pizzas."

She gave a slight smile and shrugged. "I guess you wouldn't forget something like that. People have been pulling that prank for years. I'm sure you can hire someone to help you out, but it won't be me. By the way, what did you do with the pizzas?" Another glimpse of the girl he'd known.

She'd always been curious.

"I kept one and had the others delivered to a church that feeds the poor."

"That was nice of you."

"I am nice. If you'd only give me a chance to prove it."

"If you say so." She gave him a hard stare. "Don't you have security to help with this sort of thing?"

"Of course, Congress has security. But it's more concerned with safety in the Capitol Building. They don't provide individual security for us. If we want that, we have to pay for it."

"Well, you can afford it."

"True. And I went to a friend in the FBI. He shut down my social media pages for me, but agreed with you about it being a prank. But when we shut down the page, they started emailing the pictures to me."

"Your email address is probably public information."

"I have accounts connected for work and for my constituents. But my personal email is set up on a completely different account and that's the one they're sending pictures to."

"Mmm . . . I wonder how they got that."

"I have no idea."

"What did the FBI guy say?"

"Nothing."

"Why not? I'm sure they'd be very concerned if they knew you were being stalked."

"I haven't told them."

"Why not? It seems the logical thing to do."

"When I try to save them, they disappear. When I try to forward the emails, they disappear. I haven't even managed to print them out." He motioned with his hands as if he were a magician. "Poof. They're gone. Nobody's ever seen them but me. And my assistant."

Nikki stared at him, doubt in her gaze. "I've never heard of any such thing. And I consider myself fairly proficient at computers."

"I don't understand it either. I had a computer-tech guy check out my computers. He couldn't figure it out either. But that's why I haven't bothered the security guys again. I have nothing to show them."

"Maybe you should hire a better tech guy."

"Elizabeth — that's my assistant — says he's one of the best."

"Why do you think they're doing it?"

"I'm not sure. That's why I need you. To find out what's going on. To find out who's behind it and how serious it is."

"Why do you call it a game?"

At least Nikki was listening to him, acting as if she believed him. Maybe he still could convince her to accept his job offer. He shrugged. "For lack of a better word. But I can tell you one thing — it's not very fun."

"I think you're overreacting." She smiled at him — the fake one. "It really does sound like a prank. Send the stuff back, cancel your credit cards, and don't use the internet to buy things anymore. Problem solved."

"Once would be a prank, but this keeps happening over and over. It's been going on for months. Who knows what they'll do next?"

"I understand how this could be a problem, but I'm not getting why you need me specifically. There are plenty of other capable investigators who can help you. Especially one that focuses on cybercrimes."

"You're good at what you do." He knew that because he'd kept track of her over the years. Just in case she needed him.

"I might be good, but you can afford the best. I have no idea why you think I'm the only one who can help you." Nikki met his gaze. Her tone was serious when she spoke. "I don't have time for this, Lucas. Tell me the truth now or leave."

He rubbed his eyes and then looked at her. The moment of truth had arrived.

Should he tell her that his friends thought he was imagining the whole thing? That they thought he'd suffered some sort of breakdown. Nothing else seemed to be working. He might as well tell her the truth. "Because I need you to prove I'm not losing my mind."

4

Losing his mind.

Nikki processed his words. Her gaze roved around her office, looking for a hidden camera. Was she the one being pranked? After all, she couldn't have imagined Lucas McMann sitting in her office, let alone dropping that kind of bombshell. His announcement was just shocking enough to make her too curious for her own good. "Why would you think that?"

"Because everyone thinks I'm . . ." He leaned forward, his voice anxious. "My friends think I'm imagining it, but they're wrong. You have to believe me, Nikki. This is really happening to me. It's not a figment of my imagination."

If his friends were right, it was more serious than an overactive imagination. "Why would your friends not believe you?"

He sat quietly for a moment.

She wasn't sure if he would answer or if

he was gathering his thoughts.

Finally, he answered. "They think it's some sort of delayed reaction to my wife's murder."

In her shock and anger, she'd forgotten about that. It had happened more than a year before and been on every news station in the South for several weeks. A robbery gone wrong at a convenience store. The suspects had never been found or arrested. "I'm very sorry about your wife, Lucas."

He gave her a grim smile. "Thanks. They think I need to see a psychiatrist."

Things clicked into place. "Because you might have PTSD or something like that." Now she was beginning to understand. Were his friends right?

He nodded but said nothing.

"I take it you don't want to see one."

"I don't need a doctor. I need this sick game to be over."

Nikki replayed their conversation. He did sound paranoid. His friends knew him better than she did. Her anger turned to compassion as she looked at Lucas. This was a man in pain. A man who needed help, but what kind of help?

Her kind or a doctor's kind?

"Sometimes people around us can see things we can't see ourselves." She held up

45

her camera. "Sort of like this camera. One of the reasons I always use this is it can pick up details we don't notice at the time. So when I have a job, I trust it to pick up things I might not see at the time. A psychiatrist can do the same thing. They can help us see things clearer. Things we may not notice. There's no shame in seeing a doctor, Lucas."

"I know that. And when my wife was murdered, I did see someone. And it was very helpful. More of a spiritual counselor, but don't you see? Without proof, how could the doctor not diagnose me with some sort of paranoia?" Frustration leaked out with each word. "There's no way I can get a fair evaluation if I don't have proof."

And if he had proof, then he wouldn't need a doctor.

His convoluted reasoning made sense, sort of. Nikki prided herself on her ability to read people. But she was having trouble with this situation. "Maybe you should listen to your friends. I'm sure they care about you. Sometimes we have to trust someone else instead of ourselves."

"I don't disagree with that. In fact, that's the reason I'm thinking about running for senator. It's the right time, according to my advisors. It's not something I would choose for myself right now. But I've learned to listen to other people."

He sounded so reasonable.

"But in this situation, I'm right and they're wrong. If I wasn't living it, I'd believe it was a breakdown too. What I need is for you to prove that this . . . this game is real, and then find out who's behind it so I can put a stop to it."

"But what if it's not real?"

"But it is."

Their gazes met.

"And I know you can prove it." He was firm.

"What if I prove the opposite? Then what?"

"That won't happen. This is not a figment of my imagination."

This conversation seemed to be getting them nowhere. She wasn't even sure why she was sitting here listening to him. And yet she was.

"Don't you understand? These people are playing mind games. Trying to make me think I'm paranoid. Trying to make me think I'm doing things and not remembering it. Trying to make me think I'm unstable, not fit to be a senator."

His cell phone rang.

He pulled it from his pocket and looked

at the screen. "It's my assistant." He swirled around in his chair. "Hello, Elizabeth."

A loud voice came from the phone, but Nikki couldn't make out the words.

"Calm down, Elizabeth. I know, but it couldn't be helped." He stood up and walked outside to finish the call.

Nikki stared at the yellow sticky note. The last thing she needed was to be involved with Lucas McMann. But it didn't seem right to turn her back on him, even though he'd done that once to her at a time when she'd really needed him. Forgiving him wasn't really the point. If he really was the victim of some weird internet stalking game, it needed to be stopped. Not just for Lucas. Who knew how many other victims might be out there?

Lucas walked back in. "Sorry about that. My assistant wasn't too happy. I left without telling her."

"I'm still not getting why you're here. You must have lots of people who could help you."

"I suppose. But in the world of politics it's not always easy to know who to trust. Everyone has an agenda."

How did he know he could trust her? The old Nikki would have taken this opportunity to exact revenge. The new Nikki hoped she

48

was a better person, but the old Nikki might rise up at any minute. "And you think you can trust me?"

"I'm sure of it."

She stared at the word stuck to her screen. OK, she'd been nice and listened. She'd given sincere condolences about his wife. The woman didn't deserve to die in such a way. No one did. That should be good enough. *Right, God?* "I'm not the right person for this job. I think you should listen to your friends."

"You think I'm crazy too." He straightened up and stared at her.

"I didn't say that."

"You don't have to. I've seen that look and heard that tone of voice every time I tell people."

"I'm not saying it's not real. I'm only saying you need to accept the possibility —"

"Never mind. I thought you could help me. Guess I was wrong." Instead of sounding angry, he sounded defeated. "My apologies for interrupting your day. There's only one thing left to do. I concede. They win. I lose."

"What does that mean? Exactly how will you concede when you don't know who's responsible?"

"I won't run for Senate and no more

politics. Period. I'm done. That's probably what they want anyway. Then hopefully all of this will stop. I'll go find a mountaintop to live on. Away from people and their cameras. I'm not being passive-aggressive either." He gave her a hard look. "I cannot fight them alone, I cannot get anyone to believe me, and therefore, the only way to end their game is to concede. It has to stop. And let us pray they don't do this to other people too."

Since Nikki had known Lucas McMann, his only goal was to become President of the USA. Everything in his life was done according to his plan — well, his father's plan for him. There'd never been one misstep. Except his wife's untimely death.

"Sit down, Lucas." As soon as the words were out of her mouth, she regretted them. She didn't want to send him a mixed message, but — her cell phone rang.

It was from her sister, but a text accompanied the call with *911* in it. Their code for an emergency.

"I have to take this call."

He nodded.

"Hey, Bethany."

"She's done it again."

"What's she done this time?"

"We had an argument last night, and she

50

ran away. I thought she was in school all day. Who knows where she is? When she didn't come home, I started calling her friends. That's when I found out she didn't go to school. No one has any idea where she is. And I don't either." A sob echoed. "I'm so worried."

"Did you call her cell phone?"

"She's refusing to answer or maybe something happened to her and she can't."

"Nothing happened to her. I'm sure she's just fine." Of course Cassie wasn't answering her phone. Kids were usually fearful after a big argument and feeling as if their parents and the world were against them. "What was the argument about?"

"A boy."

"Of course."

Lucas was watching her.

She should have asked him to leave while she talked with Bethany. She didn't want him to know anything about Cassie. Too late now.

"Maybe she'll answer if you call her," Bethany said.

"I'll try that as soon as we get off the phone."

"I'll hang up right now. Then call me back."

"Will do." Nikki scrolled through the

51

names on her cell phone. She looked at Lucas. "Family problems."

"We all have those, don't we? Is there anything I can do?"

Nikki shook her head as she pressed call. It rang until it went to voice mail. On her third try, she left Cassie a very pointed message to call her mother. Then she called Bethany back. "She didn't answer my call either. Did you call the police?"

"No, I don't want to get her in trouble. If I call the police, they might put her in juvie. They threatened to last time."

She hated giving advice about Cassie to her sister. "Neither do I, but it might be time for her to face the consequences of her actions. Instead of letting her get away with all this nonsense."

"I know. That's what Ray tells me all the time. But . . ." Her voice trailed off. "Maybe we should tell her the truth."

It wasn't the first time they'd had this conversation, but there was no way she was having it in front of Lucas. "I can't really discuss this right now. I'm with a client."

It didn't stop Bethany. "She must suspect something. It has to be the reason why she's so unhappy."

"She's not unhappy — she's a teenager."

"I don't know, Nikki. It seemed like the

right thing back then, but . . ."

"No buts. We'll talk about this later."

"But —" Bethany sniffled.

"But nothing." Nikki squeezed her eyes shut. "I'll try calling her again. And if she doesn't answer, I'll see if I can get a location on her phone from a friend. If we don't know where she is by morning, I'll fly home."

"You would do that?"

"Of course. I love her too." There was an uncomfortable silence for a moment. Nikki could practically read her sister's mind.

"I didn't mean it like that." Bethany's voice was quiet. "Thanks, Nikki. I don't know what I'd do without you, even though you're the little sister."

"We're family. Call me if you hear from her. I don't care what time it is, OK? But right now, I have to go. I'm with a . . . a client." She ended the call.

"So you'll take the job?" Lucas looked hopeful for the first time since he'd told her everything.

"Why would you think that?"

"You told your sister you were with a client."

"I misspoke."

"Kinda figured that. But I figured it couldn't hurt to try. So what's wrong?"

53

"My niece took a vacation without telling her parents."

"How old is she?"

She did not want to discuss Cassie with Lucas. "She's a teenager."

"So you'll go back to Maiden to look for her."

"It seems so. If she doesn't show up by morning."

"I can fly you back."

"I can handle this."

"I know you can, but I can get you there a lot quicker." He smiled and held his hands up in surrender. "No strings attached. I promise."

She'd do everything in her power to keep Cassie safe. Including a quick, silent prayer. But accepting his help could put Cassie in more jeopardy than ever.

She stood up. "Thanks, but no thanks, Lucas. And now I've got things to do. I don't mean to be rude, but . . ." Nikki picked up her camera and then held the door open for Lucas to leave.

A sad look crossed his face, but he nodded. "Thanks for listening anyway. Come on, I can get you to Maiden in record time. I flew down here, so my plane's at the airport. No strings attached, I promise. I'll find another way to deal with my own problems." As he walked out the door, he touched her arm.

Her heart ached for him. He did need help, but . . . but she just couldn't do it.

From the parking lot, a woman lifted a camera and snapped.

5

"Hey, what are you doing?" Nikki yelled.

The woman snapped another picture and then turned. Her walk turned into a jog.

Nikki pushed past Lucas. "Stop. I only want to talk to you."

"I can't. It's against the rules." The woman opened a car door and jumped in.

Nikki ran faster. What rules? What did that even mean?

Lucas sprinted past her.

The car jerked forward.

"Stop her, Lucas. We need to talk to her."

He jumped in front of the grill, but the car swerved around him and surged forward. Nikki took a picture right before it disappeared from view. Tapping the screen on the camera, she enlarged the picture. The license plate was smeared with mud. There was no way to identify that woman or her car.

Lucas walked up. "Well, do you believe

me now?"

"It would be a little hard not to. Did you hear her? She said it was against the rules. I . . . I don't know what to say."

"Say you'll help me?"

Just looking at him brought forth all sorts of emotions she'd rather not deal with — or even think about. He was the first man she'd loved and the first to break her heart. But he needed help. "We can talk about it while you fly me up to North Carolina. If you were serious about that."

He grinned. "That's a start."

"I need to make a quick stop at my apartment. Then we can be on our way."

"Sounds good."

Twenty minutes later, Nikki unlocked the door to her place. "It's not much, but it's home."

"And a home is a wonderful thing. I'm sure it's lovely."

"Not really." She opened the door. "I'm not much for decorating. Too busy."

They walked in.

He looked around the apartment. Nothing on the walls. No pictures. Just the furniture, a TV, and a few old newspapers. It looked more like a motel room than a home. "I like minimalist."

"Always the politician, aren't you?"

"It's second nature to me."

She looked longingly at the sofa. It had been an exhausting day. She turned to Lucas. "I'll pack a few things and then we can go. Make yourself comfortable. You might even find an apple in the fridge if you're hungry."

"We can go through the drive-thru on the way to the airport." Lucas sat on the sofa.

As she packed, her mind swirled. There was no doubt Lucas had a problem. Now that she'd seen it with her own eyes, she couldn't just turn her back on him. But this was an impossible situation.

But it seemed as if this was a God thing, this business of forgiveness.

If someone had asked her before today, she'd have told them Lucas McMann was a closed chapter in her life. A lesson learned. Nothing but a distant memory. Boy, had she been wrong. She'd been shocked at the intensity of her feelings when she'd seen him.

That anger couldn't be a good thing. Her Christian mentor kept telling her forgiveness was about letting go of the anger, not about letting the person she was angry with off the hook.

Maybe it was time to try God's way, which was better than her way.

She wasn't sure she could, but she was ready to give it a shot. She zipped up the bag and walked out into the living room.

Lucas sat in a chair. His eyes were closed.

"It's very nice of you to fly me to Maiden." She sat down in a chair.

He smiled as he opened his eyes. "It's not a problem. I haven't seen my mother in a while, so I can help you and make her happy at the same time. A win-win situation."

"I know you said there were no strings attached, but when I get this family situation resolved, I'll do the best I can to figure out what's going on. Then we can stop it."

"I would love for you to do that, but I don't want you to think that you have to because I'm flying you to Maiden. I told you there were no strings attached, and that's what I meant. I gave you my word . . . as a Christian."

"You're a Christian?" Of course, he had known the words to the Christian praise songs on the radio. She should have figured that one out. Some detective she was. "I only became one a few months ago. It's made a huge difference in my life. I'm so . . . I'm not sure how to explain it. All I can say is I'm happier than I've been in a long time. But I still have a long way to go."

"It's really not all that hard. Just love God

and love others. If you can do that, you'll be fine."

"Easier said than done."

"That's for sure, but God has a way of getting us to the right people when we are in need. I think that's why your name popped into my head as I was praying about this situation."

Could Lucas be right? Could she be the answer to his prayers — to anyone's prayers? It didn't seem possible after all her mistakes.

"I can't thank you enough for agreeing to help me."

"No problem." Nikki didn't think she'd actually forgiven him yet — but some of the anger was gone. Agreeing to help Lucas was a first step. It certainly wasn't because she wanted to see him. Just seeing him sent her into a tizzy. She didn't like tizzies. Memories pushed their way to the surface. Nikki shut them out. The past couldn't be changed, so why dwell on it? She stood up. "Well, let's get this show on the road, shall we?"

"Sounds like a plan." He grinned, took a pen and a checkbook from his pocket, and wrote something with a flourish. After he tore the check out and set it on her coffee table, he looked up. "Speaking of plans, do you have one?"

"I'll become your very best stalker. By following you, I should be able to spot your other stalkers. I'll take some of my own pictures and then ID them. Then I can talk with them. One of them will tell us the truth."

"How can you be so sure of that?"

She had no idea, but she wasn't going to admit it. "I have my ways."

"That sounds good, Nikki. I like it. I knew you were the right person for the job."

"I guess so."

"I can't tell you how much this means to me."

"It's not personal, Lucas. I would try to help anyone who came to me with this kind of problem."

"So what do you want me to do?"

"Go home and act normal. I'll take care of the rest."

"I don't know what normal is anymore."

"Act like a politician."

"What do you mean?"

"Think about it. Politicians hide their private problems from the world. They have to look confident to the public, to their constituents. Be strong. Be confident. In other words, be a politician."

"Good advice."

"I thought so. Remember, this is a job. Nothing more, nothing less. It's not personal, Lucas."

Their gazes met. The moment stretched out.

"I know that. Still, I can't thank —"

"You don't have to keep saying it. I heard you the other five times. And besides, I haven't done anything yet. Let's see if I can actually solve the case first." As Nikki was closing the door, the intercom buzzed. She walked back in and pressed down on the talk button. "Hello."

"It's me."

Unbelievable. One problem solved, but now she had an even bigger problem — how to get rid of Lucas?

Lucas turned back.

The blood had drained from Nikki's face and her expression was panicked. Nikki stared at the intercom. "Stay there. I'll be down in a minute. Don't move." Even her voice was shaky.

"Who was that?"

"That's my niece."

Then why wasn't she happy? Her worry had come through loud and clear during the phone conversation with her sister. "That's wonderful. All's well that ends well, right?"

She smiled — a forced one. "Absolutely,

just a little shocked. I had no idea she'd come here. It never even occurred to me."

"It's a good thing we hadn't left yet."

"I guess I won't be needing that flight to Maiden after all."

He could have used some time with Nikki to talk about the events of the past few months. It would be nice to confide in someone who actually believed him. "I can fly you both back. It will be a little crowded but still safe."

"No. No. No." She shook her head as if she were a bobble doll. "Not necessary. I . . . we . . . I'll figure something out."

She was definitely weirded out about something. Maybe it wasn't her niece downstairs waiting, but why would she lie?

"It's not a problem at all. I'll get you there a lot quicker. Might be fun for your niece. What was her name again?"

"Cassie. Cassie Martin. Don't worry, I'll still take your case. I promised and I will."

"That didn't even occur to me. I trust you. Don't you think you should go get her before she runs away again?"

"Why would she do that?"

"It was a joke, Nikki."

"Oh, yeah. Thanks for your offer, but it's not necessary. I'll drive. It will be better if I have my car in DC anyway."

"Are you sure?"

"I am and I know this will sound a bit strange, but can you go out the back entrance? If you walk across the street, you'll be able to catch a taxi. I think it would be better if no one knew I was working for you."

Most people were excited for friends and family to meet him. After all, he was a little bit famous — at least in North Carolina. "Why?"

"I think it would be better if Cassie didn't see you. She's a teenager. They are sometimes a little too curious about things that are none of their business. I don't think it would be good for this to get out. Do you?"

"I suppose not. She sounds just like her aunt. I remember you were always way too curious. Must be what took you into the detective business."

"Could be. It's better if she doesn't know I'm working for you. Or it might be posted all over the internet. She'd promise not to tell anyone, but she'd tell her best friend, and before you know it, it would have gone viral."

"Yeah, that wouldn't be so good."

The intercom buzzed.

Nikki pushed the button. "I'll be there in a minute."

"What's the problem?"

"Nothing. Just hold."

"OK."

Nikki turned back to him. "Do you think you'll be able to find a way back to the airport? I'm really sorry about this."

"I'm sure I can manage." He grinned. "I got down here, didn't I?"

"Great. I'll be in DC in a few days. But I won't be in contact with you. You go about your life and I'll be watching and waiting. If you see me, don't talk to me."

"Makes sense."

"I need your home address."

Nodding, he handed her a business card and gave her a thumbs-up. "Looking forward to it."

"Remember, if you see me, ignore me. Do not talk to me. This will only work if people don't know that we know each other."

"Will do."

Nikki stopped at a door. "Here's the steps. If you don't mind waiting for a few minutes, I'll go get Ca— my niece."

"Not a problem."

"I'll be in contact with you in a few days. In the meantime, just do what you do. And don't order any pizzas." She walked towards the elevator.

Lucas made his way down the steps. He

looked at his watch and sat down. Five minutes should be enough time for Nikki to retrieve . . . whoever it was. Maybe it wasn't her niece at all.

That could explain why she'd acted so strange. He had no idea what other cases she might be involved with. He sent up a prayer for her safety and waited some more. He respected Nikki enough to do what she'd asked.

6

When the elevator door closed, Nikki was able to breathe. There was no way she wanted Cassie in the same room as Lucas. The thought made her slightly sick. Good thing he lived in DC.

The elevator door opened.

At fifteen, Cassie was already taller than Nikki. She had none of the Kent coloring. Instead of blonde, her hair was fiery red. Unlike most redheads, her complexion had no freckles. Instead, she had a beautiful ivory skin tone that made most teenage girls envious. And those pale blue eyes.

The exact shade she'd stared into earlier. *Beautiful* was the only word to describe her daugh— niece. Cassie was her sister's daughter. They had the birth certificate to prove it. And now that their parents were dead, only three people knew the truth. Nikki, her sister, and her brother-in-law. And it would stay that way.

"Cassie."

Cassie turned to her with a sunny smile. "Auntie Nikki." Cassie ran to her.

Nikki hugged her. "How did you get here?"

"Don't ask questions unless you want to know the answer."

"Oh, but I do want to know."

Cassie did a hair flip. "Doesn't matter. I'm here safe and sound."

"We'll talk about it later. You are not off the hook, little miss." Nikki didn't want to get into an argument, but she wouldn't let Cassie think what she'd done was all right either. "Why didn't you answer my calls?"

"I was so close I wanted to surprise you."

It was a day full of surprises.

"Your mother's very worried."

A little smirk appeared on Cassie's face.

"That is not nice. Your parents love you very much. There's no reason to torment them the way you do." Nikki stabbed the up button.

"I'm not tormenting them." Cassie shrugged. "Not really."

They stepped into the elevator.

"One of these days, you'll go too far and get yourself hurt." Nikki's eyes filled with tears. This was ridiculous — she needed to get control over her emotions. She turned towards the elevator panel and hit the number three.

"No need to worry about me, Auntie. I can take care of myself. Just like you can."

Nikki's heart skipped a beat. Maybe Bethany was right. Maybe Cassie did suspect. "Oh, really? So, you've been trained by the Army in hand-to-hand combat? I didn't realize that."

Cassie rolled her eyes. "I just meant —"

"I know what you meant. And you are very wrong. You can't take care of yourself. It's way too dangerous for you to have hitchhiked here."

"I didn't hitchhike. Do you think I'm that stupid?"

"No, but you're like most kids — you think bad things can't happen to you. But they can." Nikki unlocked her door and motioned with a sweep of her arm in a dramatic fashion. "Welcome to my new apartment, my dear niece."

Cassie smiled as she skipped past her. "I knew you were glad to see me."

"Always." Nikki picked up her home phone off the end table. "Call your mother. Now."

"I'm really tired. I'll do it later."

"You will call her right after you tell me how you got here."

Cassie walked through the apartment, opening doors and peeking in the rooms. "You should have more faith in me. I didn't do anything dangerous. There's no bed in the spare room. Where am I supposed to sleep?"

Nikki ignored her question. "I'll be the judge of that. How did you get here?"

"My friend's brother is a truck driver. I asked him for a ride. No big deal."

"That wasn't the best of ideas. He may have had other ideas in mind."

"No way. He's an old dude. As old as you."

"Thanks for calling me old."

"You know what I meant." She flopped down on the sofa. "I answered your question. Now answer mine."

"What?"

"Where am I supposed to sleep?"

"The same place all uninvited guests sleep." Nikki pointed at the sofa.

"No problem. That's still more comfortable than that crummy truck. You can't imagine how bumpy the ride was."

"Serves you right."

"I'm hungry."

"We'll eat after you call your mother." Nikki pointed at the phone.

Cassie rolled her eyes but picked up the

phone. "OK, but I'm starving."

"You call her while I stick a frozen pizza in the oven."

"Extra cheese."

"I know." Nikki walked back into the living room after she loaded the pizza.

Cassie was lying on the sofa with the phone to her ear. "I know, Mom. I said I was sorry. I just got so mad — no, don't put Dad . . . hi, Dad."

Cassie's expression said her father's end of the conversation wasn't good. With another roll of her eyes, she handed the phone to Nikki and headed off to the kitchen.

"Hi, Ray."

"I'll pay for a bus ticket. Put her on the bus tomorrow morning."

"No need. I'll drive her home. I have a job in DC, so it's on my way."

"What kind of a job?"

"Client privilege, remember?"

"That's for attorneys and doctors, not for private investigators, Nikki." A pause. "I can only think of one person we know in Washington, DC. Do you really think that's wise?"

Ray was way too smart. No wonder he'd become a doctor.

"It's a long, complicated story, and besides, I gave my word."

Cassie walked back in.

"I can't really talk about it now. But I know what I'm doing. Want to say goodbye to your daughter?" She handed the device to Cassie as the girl vehemently shook her head no.

Cassie made a face as she took the phone. She followed Nikki into the kitchen. After Cassie hung up, she took a deep, appreciative sniff. "Pizza smells great. I'm starving. The guy wouldn't stop for any reason, and all he had in the truck to eat was some stale donuts."

"Were."

"Were what?"

"Were some stale donuts. All he had in the truck were some stale donuts. Good English is important. And it serves you right for pulling a stunt like that. You deserved nothing better than stale donuts."

Nikki plopped a few pieces onto each of their plates. The extra cheese oozed. It did smell wonderful. It had been a long time since she'd eaten.

They moved into the living room.

Once Cassie was settled in, she looked at Nikki. "Do you have a pool?"

"It doesn't matter. We're leaving in the morning."

"Where are we going?"

"Where do you think?"

Cassie glared at her. "I came all this way to have some fun. With my favorite auntie. Not to go straight back home."

"If you think I'll reward you for bad behavior, you are very wrong, little miss. But if you promise to be good for the rest of the school year, we can talk to your parents about summer vacation."

"Really. That would be awesome. The whole summer in Florida. Everyone will be so jealous."

"I did not say the whole summer. A week or two. I do have to work, you know."

Cassie swallowed her last bite of pizza and then stood up. "I need more. You want some?"

Nikki shook her head. "I'm good."

A moment later, Cassie walked back in with another plate full of pizza. She set her plate on the coffee table. Her gaze moved from Nikki and landed on the check — the check with Lucas McMann's name.

Nikki fought the urge to grab it up, but that would only cause more curiosity. Instead, she took a bite of pizza, praying Cassie wouldn't pick up the check.

But she did.

"Don't," Nikki said. "That's private. It's

from a client and —"

Cassie unfolded the check. "Wow. That's a lot of money."

"Cassie, that is confidential. Give it to me." She put out her hand and waited.

"I had no idea you made that kind of money from being a private investigator. Who can afford that?"

"None of your business. Give me the check."

Cassie looked down. "Lucas McMann. That congressman from Maiden? What's he want with you?" She placed the check in Nikki's waiting hand.

"None of your business." She smiled to take the sting out of her words. "It's private."

"Come on, you can tell me. I won't tell anyone. What's he want you to do? Find some love child from his past?"

"Cassie! Don't be ridiculous." Nikki rolled her own eyes for emphasis. "It's nothing like that. It's a private matter."

Cassie picked up her plate. "What fun are you? You probably have a really juicy story."

"It's actually something odd, but I respect his privacy. You should do the same."

"Boring. I didn't even know you knew him."

"He was older than me, but you know

Maiden. Everyone knows everyone."

"Isn't that the truth? Did Mom and Dad know him too?"

"Probably. They were closer in age to him. I don't know if they were friends or not. Now, don't think distracting me with work will make me forget what you've done. We need to have a serious discussion about you and your choices."

Cassie sighed. "Boring."

7

The evening sky was marbled with reds and oranges and a touch of purple. Lucas breathed in the peace and tranquility. He felt closest to God when he was in this plane. Flying was therapy. The heavenly kind.

After his wife's death, he'd fly and pray and question God. The answers didn't come quickly, but they did come. God had been faithful to him through it then, and He would be faithful now. Asking Nikki to help had been the right thing to do. She'd be able to figure out what was happening.

He'd kept track of her through the years. First, the Army and then the police force. After several commendations as a police officer, she'd gone out on her own. And knowing Nikki, he could just imagine why. She was a free spirit. She didn't mind following rules, but she probably found out rather quickly that there was a rigid and

76

oftentimes political framework in law enforcement. It was always a struggle between the constituents they protected and the city hall who governed them.

After becoming a private investigator, Nikki had a few high-profile cases as well. She was good at her job. She'd be able to help him.

Coming into Maiden, he flew above his family home. Even from this distance, it still had the air of gracious Southern living. White pillars adorned the large Civil War–era house. Wrought-iron gates. The mandatory stable and tennis courts. And the swimming pool. That was one thing he'd enjoyed as a child — and so had his friends.

He'd detested the house growing up. Too big. Too formal. Too many expectations, especially from his father. But his mother still lived there, and it was now his official residence. He'd sold his house after Victoria's death and moved into the guesthouse.

After landing the plane, he hopped out. He could take the golf cart up to the house, but the exercise would do him good. It had been a stressful day. Now that Nikki had agreed to help, he was a bit more optimistic.

The quiet and the night air worked their magic as he walked towards the guesthouse.

His tense muscles relaxed, but he couldn't get his mind off Nikki.

Why had he allowed his father to break them up? What would have happened if their relationship had been allowed to run its natural course? Would they have gone their separate ways when he went to college or would they have made it work? Not that it mattered — he wasn't looking for romance.

After Victoria's death, he'd recommitted himself to his work. To the plan to become President of the United States. Now even that was at risk.

He stared at the guesthouse — his home now. There wouldn't be a speck of food in there and he was hungry. He'd sneak up to the main house and surprise his mother. He walked up to the back door. Hitting numbers on the security keypad, he smiled at the modern convenience. His mother hadn't been happy when he and his sister had insisted on it after his father's death but she had acquiesced to their wishes.

A small night-light shone from the kitchen counter. He walked to the refrigera—

"Mister, don't make another move. I don't know who you are, but I suggest you turn yourself around and skedaddle before I shoot you."

"Mama, it's me, Lucas."

"Oh, my goodness. Lucas." A moment later, light flooded the kitchen. His mother stood in the doorway with a shotgun pointed at him and her silver hair askew. "I didn't realize it was you. Sorry."

"Put that gun away, Mama."

With a sheepish smile, she leaned it against the kitchen wall. "Well, how was I supposed to know it was you down here skulking around like some thief in the night? A single woman needs to protect herself, you know." She smoothed her hair.

He arched a brow. "With a double-barreled 12 gauge?"

"It was good enough for my daddy and it's good enough for me."

"You can't be walking around with that thing. You're either going to kill yourself or someone else."

"That's the point."

"Mama —"

"If you think I'll let some thief just walk in and do what he wants, you're sadly mistaken. And I won't argue about it. I may be old, but I can still take care of myself. It is so good to see you." She crooked a finger and then put her arms around him. "You should have called."

"I know. But it was a spur-of-the-moment trip."

She stepped back. "You don't do spur-of-the-moment."

He couldn't deny the truth of her words. "A man can change."

She looked at him over her glasses. "Not that much. Elizabeth called here looking for you earlier. She was beside herself that you'd missed your appointment with the senator. But when you hadn't shown up by bedtime, I figured you'd gone somewhere else."

He certainly wouldn't tell her where he'd been or who he'd seen. "What did you tell her?"

"What could I tell her? The truth. You haven't been here in months. And that I hadn't heard from you since you called last Sunday. She seemed worried."

"I already explained to her I needed a few days to myself. She shouldn't have called here bothering you."

"It was no bother. What's going on, Lucas?"

"Nothing, Mama. Why would you ask that?"

"Humph. The better question is why you can't look me in the eye when you say nothing's wrong." She pointed at the marble kitchen island. "Sit down. I'll fix you some scrambled eggs. I assume that's why you were sneaking into my kitchen in the middle of the night. Looking for something to eat."

"It's not the middle of the night, Mama."

"It is for this old lady."

"You don't have to cook. I'm more than capable of finding something to eat."

She pointed once again. "Sit."

He grinned and slid onto the stool. "I am a bit hungry."

A few minutes later, she placed the scrambled eggs in front of him, filled with all his favorites — cheese, onions, hot peppers, mushrooms, red and green peppers. A moment later, toast and orange juice appeared.

"Looks delicious, Mama."

She nodded and sat down. After he ate a few bites, she smiled and said, "Now tell me what's wrong."

Should he tell her? Probably not — it would only worry her. "Delicious. The best scrambled eggs ever."

"Don't think I don't know you're avoiding my question. Elizabeth told me you not only missed your appointment but a vote today as well. You wouldn't do that unless you had a very good reason."

He set down his fork. "Mama, I won't insult you by telling you nothing's wrong.

But I can handle it. In fact, I am handling it. I have a plan that's already in motion."

"A plan. Well, that sounds promising. So why exactly are you here then?"

"To visit my mama, of course. And it's time for me to get my act together. Time to stop feeling sorry for myself." He stabbed a piece of pepper. "Someone told me to start acting like a politician today."

"Sounds like a very smart person to me."

"To me too, Mama." After saying good night to his mother, Lucas walked into the guesthouse. His home away from home. He looked around. It didn't feel much like home in spite of his mother's efforts. But then again, nowhere did these days. Victoria had been his home, and now she was gone. "I'm sorry, Victoria. I should have kept you safe."

Maybe the game master had the right idea. Maybe he should resign from politics.

He walked through the tiny living room to the spare bedroom — his office when he was here. He stared at the laptop. It was late and he knew he shouldn't turn it on. If he did, he'd be up for hours. And now that he'd left without notice, there would be a ton of work waiting. He'd check his email and that would be it. He needed to get some sleep. Lucas scrolled through the list. His throat constricted when he saw the subject line listed as *MUST SEE.*

Not again.

Ignore it. If he opened it, he probably wouldn't get any sleep. Curiosity won. As the picture loaded, he broke out in a sweat. Behind him in the picture was a window with the logo *Kent Investigations.* And right next to him stood Nikki. It didn't matter how hard he tried to hide, they would find him. His gaze moved downward. He read the caption.

SOMEONE WILL DIE IF YOU REPEAT THE SAME MISTAKE TWICE!

Who would die? Nikki? Himself? What mistake? And why did they think he was about to repeat it? He had no idea what the warning meant. This wasn't suggestive of danger — it was blatant. Were they serious? Surely not.

The game master wanted to freak him out. And he'd succeeded.

He pulled out the business card Nikki had given him and forwarded the email to her. Would she actually get it? Probably not. No one else ever did.

After he sent the email, he hit the icon of the print button. Nothing happened. It wasn't on. He jumped up and moved to the printer, plugging it in and then turning it on. The red light blinked off and the green one blinked on. He hurried back to the computer.

The screen was blank. The picture was gone — just like all the other times.

He pulled out his cell phone and dialed Nikki. It rang several times and then went to voice mail. "Nikki, this is Lucas. I received another email. I sent it to you. Let me know if you got it."

Had he put Nikki in danger by going to her for help? Was that what the message meant? He wouldn't take that chance. He'd tell her that her services were no longer needed. He'd have to hire someone else or deal with it alone. He slammed a fist into the desk. Knowing it was hopeless, he went through file after file, trying to find the email. But it was gone. Had Nikki received the email?

He pulled out his phone and hit her number. It rang several times and then went to voice mail again. He started to leave a message. What if they were listening? He hadn't thought of that. Did they have some sort of bug installed in his phone? His mind flashed through some of the conversations he'd had. Crucial information was often discussed. Matters of national importance. He'd need to have the phone checked out

84

tomorrow. Why hadn't he thought of that before? Because he was too frazzled. Too emotional to be clearheaded. He hit the end button.

Was he being ludicrous? They already knew he'd been in contact with Nikki. Was that the mistake they referred to in the email? Were they warning him not to involve anyone else in their game?

Maybe he should resign. He'd threatened to do that at Nikki's office. The more he thought about it, the more reasonable it sounded. Quitting would be worth it if they left him alone. If they left Nikki alone.

They'd said not to make the same mistake twice. Nikki was the first investigator he'd hired. So that couldn't be what they meant.

He called Nikki's number again and left another message. He didn't tell her the picture was of her office. She could look at it and come to her own conclusions as to whether it was a valid threat. It was only after he'd hung up that he realized he'd not told her he was in Maiden, rather than Washington, DC.

He paced around the room. His phone rang. "Hello, Elizabeth. What can I do for you?"

"Lucas, I wanted to know when you'd be back to work. Should I cancel your appointments for next week?"

Nikki said that she would be in DC next week. He had to be there so she could do her work.

"Don't cancel them. I'll be back Monday."

"If you're sure."

"I'm sure."

"Where did you say you were?"

"I didn't say." He trusted Elizabeth, but he wouldn't tell her where he was in case they were listening. Of course, they probably knew anyway. "See you on Monday." He clicked off before she could ask him another question.

Nikki probably wouldn't call back until morning.

Lucas decided to call it a night. As he climbed into bed, he pushed the ringer up to full volume in case Nikki called back. He'd tell her about the warning then.

Lucas woke up, surprised that he'd actually fallen asleep. He'd tossed and turned most of the night. He grabbed the phone.

Maybe Nikki hadn't received the voice message or the email.

He rang her number again.

No answer.

He left a simple voice message this time. "Call me." Jumping out of bed, he moved directly to the computer. After scrolling the new emails, he breathed easier. No new ones from the game master. He thought back to last night's email. In the light of day, it seemed more like a prank. Nothing the game master had done had ever been threatening before. So maybe this email wasn't from him.

Still, Lucas couldn't take that chance. He would tell Nikki her services were no longer needed when she called him back. After he showered, he headed up to the main house. His mother was in the kitchen. "Morning, Mama."

"Morning? It's practically afternoon."

He checked his watch. "Mama, it's barely five minutes after nine. I would hardly call that afternoon."

"In my day, people didn't waste the day by sleeping it away." She grinned. "Ready for some pancakes?"

"Stop pulling my leg, Mama. You know how much I love those."

"I do. That's why I mixed up a batch." She picked up a bowl sitting on the counter.

"Got pecans in there?"

"Of course."

"Then pancakes sound like a marvelous idea."

The batter sizzled as she spooned it onto

the griddle.

Lucas got the maple syrup and two plates. He poured a cup of coffee. "Want a cup?"

"I would love a cup, but my doctor says one cup a day is all I get. And I had that hours ago."

"Not everyone gets up with the chickens."

"Maybe they should. Everyone would get a lot more accomplished if they did." She walked over with a platter full of pecan pancakes. "You know what would be another marvelous idea?"

He speared two with his fork. "What would that be, Mama?" He reached for the syrup.

She didn't speak for a few moments as she readied her own plate. "That you tell me what's going on, Lucas."

"Can't I just be home for a visit?"

"Of course you can, but I don't think that's what's happening here."

"Why not?"

"Call it mother's intuition."

"I told you last night that I can handle the situation. The situation isn't why I'm here." He grinned. "I suddenly had a hankering for some maple-pecan pancakes."

"So you say."

"Can't a man miss his mama?"

She gave him a look as she took another

dainty bite of pancake. "What's on your agenda for the day?"

"Not a whole lot. I thought I'd drive down to Hickory and show my face at the mall. Shake some hands. Show people I'm still alive and kicking. Then later come back to Maiden and make a few stops around town."

"Why don't you call your sister? Suzie loves the mall. That way, it will look a little more natural to people. I wouldn't want them to think you just went there to be seen."

"You need to take over as my campaign manager."

"If I did, would you tell me what's going on?"

8

Cassie was slouched on the passenger seat, her mouth hanging open and little purring sounds emanating.

Nikki smiled. Just the kind of photo she would hate. Picking up her phone from the console, she snapped a few. She didn't mind that Cassie had spent most of the drive sleeping. It gave her time to think and to pray. It was still hard to believe she'd agreed to help Lucas.

She checked her phone. Lucas had called again. There was no way to check her voice mail with Cassie so close. She'd call him back as soon as she dropped Cassie off.

Cassie opened her eyes. "What are ya doing?"

"Nothing. Glad to see you awake. What happened to helping me stay awake?"

Cassie grinned. "I'm a growing girl. I need my rest." She straightened up and looked around. "Hey, we're in Maiden."

"So we are. You woke up just in time."
Nikki pulled into her sister's drive. She
pointed at Cassie. "You — get in there and
face the consequences. And be nice about it
or no visit this summer. Got it?"

Cassie rolled her eyes, but grinned. "Got
it." She grasped the door handle. "Aren't
you coming in with me?"

"No way. You're on your own. I'll be back
later."

"Thanks for all your support, Auntie."

"My pleasure, sweetie. Hopefully, next
time, you'll think twice before pulling a
stunt like this."

"Probably not."

Nikki glared at her.

Cassie shrugged. "What? I'm just being
truthful."

Nikki drove off with a smile. In spite of
Cassie making some wrong choices, she was
growing into a sweet young lady. And nothing she'd said on the drive made Nikki think
Cassie had an inkling about who her bio
parents were. Bethany should relax about
that.

After parking on Main Street, Nikki
walked into her favorite restaurant in her
hometown. Nothing much changed in
Maiden, North Carolina. And that's how
her citizens liked it. And so did Nikki, even

though she wasn't technically a citizen. In her heart, Maiden would always be home.

The old-fashioned diner had been an actual dining car at some time.

Picking up a menu, Nikki hurried to the only empty booth.

The waitress walked over. "Are you ready? If not, I can come back in a few."

"The chicken-fried steak, but I want chicken gravy instead of the white. Mashed potatoes and a diet soda."

"Got it."

"Thanks, Misty."

The waitress looked up from her order pad. "Well, as I live and breathe, if it ain't Nikki Kent. Sorry I didn't recognize you. It's as busy as a mall on Christmas Eve here today."

"Don't worry about it. We can catch up later if it slows down."

"Not too slow, I hope." Misty touched the pocket of her apron. "I need my tips. It won't take too long for your food."

"Thanks." Nikki's gaze moved to the door as the tinkling of the bell announced a new patron. The blood rushed to her face. He was supposed to be in DC. She hadn't seen Lucas in sixteen years and now twice in a week. Maybe he was the one stalking her. Obviously not. He hadn't noticed she was in the restaurant yet.

Lucas walked up to the customers in the first booth and gave a sunny smile. "Hi. I'm Lucas McMann, the congressman for this district." He schmoozed his way through the diner.

She'd been too busy yesterday being angry to take notice. He'd aged. No longer a boy, his brown hair had been replaced with some silver. He still had that sexy grin and those pale blue eyes that reminded her of a North Carolina sky after a hard rain. No wonder he kept getting reelected for every position he ran for. Voters loved a handsome politician. And as much as she hated to admit it, Lucas was that. Not that she cared.

"So, how are you fine folks today?" he asked the customers in the booth next to hers.

Lucas glanced at her and then back at the people, but a second later, he focused back on her. A slow smile as he nodded while the woman in the booth told him exactly what she thought about the terrible condition of the state's roads.

He straightened up. "I know what you mean, ma'am. And I promise to look into the matter."

"Sounds as if you have the right idea, Congressman. Take care of the roads and I might just vote for you."

"I'll do my best. It was nice to meet you." He walked to Nikki's booth with his hand held out. "Lucas —"

"So I heard." She glared at him, hoping he would get her hidden message. *Go away.* "I don't vote."

"That's OK. I'm here to get a bite to eat at my favorite restaurant. Is it all right with you if I sit here? Doesn't seem to be any other seats available."

She had told him not to talk to her if he saw her. But that was in DC. He must think it was all right here. But it wasn't. He either hadn't gotten her message, or more likely, chose to ignore it. She nodded. "I suppose."

"Thank you so much. And I promise, no politics."

"Not likely."

"Such a cynic." Instead of sitting in the empty side, he sat down beside her, giving her no choice but to scoot over as he slid into the booth. "If you don't like politics, what do you like?"

"None of your business."

Misty walked over with a huge platter in her hand. A lake of chicken gravy decorated the mashed potatoes and the crispy battered steak. She leaned past Lucas and set the platter down. "Here you go, Nikki."

"That looks wonderful. Thanks, Misty."

Lucas smiled at the waitress. "Oh, that looks good enough to eat. I'll have the same. Only I want the white gravy."

"Nice to see you again, Congressman McMann."

"Call me Lucas, please."

Misty pulled out her order pad and wrote his order down. "And to drink?"

"Coffee — black."

"Anything else?"

"Oh, yeah. I'll have one of your famous berry cobblers. And make that à la mode, please."

Misty smiled. "You want the cobbler after your meal, I'm assuming."

"You know what. I think not. Bring it out while the other is cooking."

"Really?"

"Sure, why not. I'll bet it will taste even better while I'm starving."

"Will do." Misty walked away, shaking her head.

"Do you eat like that all the time? If so, I'm surprised you don't weigh five hundred pounds."

His voice went down a notch or two. "Not at all. But it will make a great story for all the patrons to tell. Word of mouth is the best publicity there is."

95

"You sound like a politician."

"Well, you're the one who told me to start acting like one. So I am."

"So I did." She plowed into her chicken-fried steak. Delicious. After a few bites and a long sip through her straw, she looked at him. "What are you doing here? I thought you needed to go to DC."

"I postponed that. Decided the last thing I needed right now was more publicity. Elizabeth will reschedule it." He shrugged. "I figured a few days back here would do me good. Did you listen to my message?"

"Not yet. I haven't had time."

Misty walked over with a giant helping of the cobbler topped with ice cream. "Here you go, Senator." She pulled a camera out of her pocket.

He tensed.

Nikki was suddenly aware of his thigh resting against hers. It felt too familiar. She scooted away.

"Mind if I take a picture of you eating?" Misty pointed at the wall behind the counter. It was decorated with other patrons enjoying their food.

"Not at all." He picked up his spoon, scooped it full, and then moved it up to his mouth.

Misty snapped a few pictures. "We might

96

try to get it in the paper if that's all right with you."

"Have you ever known a politician to turn down publicity?"

Misty laughed. "Can't say that I have. Of course, you're the only one I know." She looked over at Nikki and then back at Lucas. Her eyes narrowed. "Hey, weren't the two of you an item at one time in high school?"

Nikki almost choked on the chicken-fried steak. She swallowed. "I wouldn't say we were an item. We dated a few times."

Lucas hid his smile. It was fun watching her squirm a bit, trying to avoid the question.

"Yeah, it seems to me that the two of you were head over heels. I mean, you don't go to the prom with just anyone. Whatever happened with the two of you anyway?"

Nikki stuffed another bite of her chicken-fried steak in her mouth even though she was coughing from the last piece.

Lucas took pity and rescued her. "Graduation happened. I went off to college while Nikki kept breaking hearts here in Maiden for a few more years."

"That's right. You were older than us."

Misty grinned. "And that silver hair proves it."

"It proves nothing except that I come from a long line of premature gray-haired men."

"It looks good on you. So . . . what's this little luncheon about?" Misty grinned.

"Just a coincidence, really. I had no idea she'd be here."

"Same here," Nikki managed to say as she reached for her soda. "Two old friends catching up. That's all."

"I don't know. The two of you look awfully cozy. Just the way you used to."

"That was all a long time ago, Misty. Please don't put that in the paper."

"I won't. But it's odd, both of you showing up here at the same time. Know what I mean?" Misty grinned.

"That's what I was just saying to Nikki. Both of us showing up in Maiden at the very same time and here at the restaurant. Serendipity, right?" Lucas winked at Misty. "It must mean something."

Misty looked at each of them with a knowing smile. "You still make a great-looking couple. It wouldn't surprise me if God has something in mind for the two of you."

Nikki's face flushed red as she protested. "That is so ridiculous, Misty. I'm a private investigator in Florida and he's about to become a US senator. God definitely has no plans for the two of us. Together."

Misty shook her head. "I'm just saying."

"Well, don't say it again. Please." Nikki set her fork down. "I am so over marriage. One time was more than enough for me. No offense, Lucas."

Misty laughed. "Amen to that, sister."

Lucas agreed wholeheartedly with them. He had no intention of ever marrying again, but a little flirting was good for the soul. He winked at Misty. "But you just never can tell what God has planned."

"That's for sure. God sure can surprise us." Misty laughed as she walked away.

"I can't believe you said that." Nikki glared at him again, this time for real. Her whisper came out as a hiss. "Why would you say such a thing? We aren't supposed to even be in contact with each other. The plan won't work if —"

"What did you want me to say?" Lucas laughed. "Besides, I didn't bring up our past. She did. I couldn't very well act as if we never saw each other before, could I? That we were complete strangers. Then she would have thought something was really odd."

"As far as I'm concerned, we are complete

strangers." She glared. "And I plan on keeping it that way."

"Don't worry. I'm quite content with being a bachelor. Romance is the last thing on my mind. Gives me more time for work." He scooped a bite of the berry cobbler into his mouth. "And like you said, I'm all about the politics."

"Good. Just don't forget it, or I will give you back your check."

"We need to talk about that." Perfect opening for what he had to say. "I don't want the check back, but I don't need your services any longer."

"Excuse me." Her eyes grew wide. "Yesterday it was so much of an emergency, you flew down to Florida to talk me into taking a case I didn't want, and now today you no longer need my services? That doesn't make sense."

"I've had some time to reflect, and I think you're right. It's probably all a prank and I'm overreacting." He forced his voice to sound casual, unconcerned. That wasn't exactly the truth, but he needed to keep Nikki safe.

Nikki pushed her plate away, only half-eaten. "I'm not buying it. What really happened, Lucas?"

"Nothing happened. I changed my mind.

Simple as that. Keep the check for your trouble." He scooped another bite of the cobbler into his mouth.

"What trouble? I didn't do anything to earn it. I don't need your charity, Lucas. I make a good living at what I do."

"I know that. It's just easier for my accountant if you accept the check. Donate it to your favorite charity if you want."

Her nails clicked on the speckled tabletop as she stared at him.

He had to make her believe that nothing was wrong. If she had an inkling that he was trying to protect her, she wouldn't be happy.

"Lucas, you were practically begging me to help you yesterday. And now all of a sudden, my services aren't needed? I don't think so. I said I'd help you. I haven't listened to your voice messages yet. Is that why you kept calling me over and over?"

Nikki was too smart for her own good.

If he told her about the message, it would only make her more insistent. She didn't seem the kind of person to back down from a fight. Or from danger. He had to come up with a plausible reason. "Not exactly."

"Then what were you calling about?"

"It wasn't all that important. I got another email yesterday and sent it to you. I just wanted to know if you'd received it."

She pulled out her phone and scrolled. Finally, she looked up. "Nope. Not one email from you."

Good. This was one time he was glad they'd messed with his computer. It would be easier to convince her to quit without her reading his panicked email. "Fine, you want the truth."

"It seems like a good idea." She sipped her soda.

"I came down to Florida to see you with the thought of, you know, renewing our friendship. After talking with you, I realized you would never be interested in even being friends, let alone more."

She stared, her mouth dropped in shock. "Just a minute ago, you said you weren't interested in romance."

He shrugged. "That might have been a slight exaggeration."

"So what? All that about being stalked was a lie?"

"Not at all. That's all true, but I can find another investigator to help me. It doesn't have to be you."

She sat there, not saying a word.

He waited for the explosion. It didn't happen.

"I can't believe you scammed me again.

And I can't believe I fell for it." Her voice was quiet, but filled with hurt. Not the anger he expected.

And that made him feel worse. But he'd have to endure it. Better that she never speak to him again than someone hurt her. He couldn't allow that to happen — wouldn't, no matter what the consequences were for himself. "It wasn't a scam, Nikki. I just left out the part that I could hire someone else. I didn't want someone else — I wanted you. That's a compliment. Not a scam."

She stood up. "Excuse me. I need to leave. And I will be sending the check back. I don't care how big of a headache it causes for your accountant."

He didn't move.

His hand covered her hand, but she shook it off. "Don't touch me. What? Did you think if you hired me, you'd get some side benefits? I wish I'd never met you." A look of sadness passed in her eyes.

"That's not true, Nikki. We meant something to each other until I messed it up. You are one of my best memories. I just wanted to see you again. What's wrong with that?"

"You do have a way with words, I'll give you that. But your words mean nothing. Just a politician schmoozing. Trying to get his

103

way once again."

Their gazes met.

She wasn't thinking about this time. Her words told him just how much he'd hurt her — now and before. Why had he capitulated to his father's demands?

"That's not true, Nikki."

"I forgive you for all of it, Lucas. Because that's what God wants me to do. But that doesn't mean I trust you. I shouldn't have trusted you then, and I sure don't trust you now. And I never will." Her words were like the clanging of a prison door.

She picked up her bill, but he grabbed it first. "I'll take care of it. It's the least I can do."

Nikki nodded. "Fine. Thank you. Let me out."

"That's it."

"That's it." In a louder voice, she said, "It was so nice to see you again, Congressman. Thanks for lunch."

9

Nikki counted to ten as she marched towards the door. How in the world had Lucas managed to suck her into his world again? And for his own selfish reasons? What was it about him that blinded her to the type of person he really was? Well, it was all over this time. Never again would she let him trick her.

A twenty-something young man stood by the cash register with his cell phone aimed at Lucas.

Nikki moved in front of him, blocking the camera.

His eyes moved from the screen to her. "Hey, get out of the way. I was taking a picture of the congressman. It's not every day I see someone famous."

"Don't you think he has a right to eat lunch in privacy?"

He ran a hand through his slightly shaggy brown hair and then shrugged. "Not really.

The Supreme Court ruled public figures have no expectation of privacy."

"A wannabe lawyer, huh?"

He glared at Nikki. "No, just someone who knows his rights."

"That's wonderful. Why don't you give him a little privacy anyway?" Even as she said the words, she realized the irony. That was what Stanley, the cheating husband, had wanted, and it hadn't bothered her in the least to take his picture. And now she was telling this guy to give Lucas some privacy.

His eyes narrowed. "Maybe the two of you have a secret you're trying to hide. Is that it? A little secret rendezvous. Don't want your little tryst to make the news, huh?" He pointed the camera at her and clicked.

"Stop that." Her hand moved in front of the camera screen. "We're not having anything. I'm just say—"

"Hey, you got no right." He shoved her out of the way.

She closed in fast. Her hand shoved him away. She whispered, but her tone left no doubt she wasn't joking. "I have no right? You sure don't have a right to put your hands on me."

From behind the register, Misty sounded panicked. "We don't want any trouble in here. Let's just calm —"

Nikki heard whispers of the other people in the restaurant. This was getting out of hand. In one swift movement, she grabbed his hand, twisted it behind his back, and pushed him towards the door. She looked at Misty. "I'll be back to take care of his check in a minute."

"Let go of me," he whined.

"Not on your life." Knowing the confrontation was her fault, she planned to go outside and apologize to him. He hadn't been doing anything wrong. This may not have been the nicest way to handle it, but a big argument in the diner wouldn't solve the problem. A problem she'd managed to cause. Outside was the place to do it.

The two stumbled down the diner steps together.

"I'm —"

As their feet hit the sidewalk, he turned and shoved her — hard. Her elbow smashed into the cement as she landed. The pain shot through her arm. *Don't react. The guy has a right to be angry.* She held up her hands. "Look, I'm sorry. I overreacted in there. I —"

His foot smashed into her stomach.

Now he'd made her mad. She jumped up, ready to attack, but before she could, Lucas grabbed him.

"That's no way to treat a lady, son."

"She ain't no lady. Didn't you see what she did to me?" He struggled to get away from Lucas without success.

Lucas appeared unfazed by the commotion. At least on the outside.

Even though she was angry, Nikki forced her voice to sound apologetic. "Look, I'm sorry. I was trying to apologize, but you hit me before I could."

People spilled out of the diner to watch. Others on the street stopped and stared. So much for keeping a low profile.

"You're the one who pushed me out of the diner."

"Look, I'm trying to apologize. I admit it was all my fault. You —"

"Funny way of apologizing. Grabbing me and pushing me out of the restaurant." His voice was petulant, reminding her of a three-year-old.

But this mess was all her fault. She needed to be gracious. Find a way to appease the guy. "I agree. I overreacted, but I didn't want to cause a ruckus in the diner." She extended a hand. "I really am sorry. And just to show you how sorry, I'm going to go back inside and pay your bill. OK? Lunch is my treat." Her gaze moved towards the alley across the street.

He shrugged. "Well, I didn't get —"

Out of the corner of her eye, she saw a man across the street. A man with a gun aimed in their direction. She pushed the kid down and then tackled Lucas to the ground as well. Her gaze stayed focused on the man.

The gunman's eyes widened for a moment before he ran.

Jumping off Lucas, Nikki sprinted across the street.

The gunman was too far ahead. She'd never be able to catch him. Forcing her legs to move faster, she cut the distance between them.

At the end of the alley, he turned right. Nikki lost sight of him. She increased her speed. This was the reason she worked out faithfully. In her job, fitness made a difference. At the end of the alley, she turned right but stopped.

No gunman.

Her gaze scanned the area.

The light turned green and a dark van drove through it. He couldn't have gotten into that van and driven away.

She was only a few seconds behind him.

Two young boys walked down the steps of the library.

She yelled across to them. "Hey, did you

boys see some guy running down the street?"

With wide eyes, they both shook their heads.

He couldn't have disappeared.

She'd seen him turn right. She walked across the street to the boys. After taking a few deep breaths, she asked, "Are you sure?"

"Nope. We didn't see no one, ma'am."

When had young boys started calling her ma'am? "Anyone."

"What?" The boy seemed confused.

" 'We didn't see no one' is not good English. It's 'we didn't see anyone.' "

"What are you? An English teacher?"

"Never mind. Are you sure you didn't see a man come out of the alley?"

"No. That van did pull away as we were coming out of the libary, but we didn't see no one . . . anyone running."

"It's library with an *r.*"

"That's what I said, ma'am. Liba*ry.*"

"How many people were in the van?"

"One."

The other boy spoke up. "No, I thought I saw another person. On the passenger side."

The first boy shrugged. "Don't know. If he says it was two, it probably was."

"OK, thanks." That van must have been waiting for the gunman. That made sense.

Two men, one in a getaway van. This whole thing seemed planned, not spur-of-the-moment. But Lucas's visit hadn't been planned. What was going on? Picture taking was one thing, but a man with a gun?

That wasn't a game.

Stunned and more than a little embarrassed, Lucas moved to a sitting position. One minute he was talking to Nikki and the kid. The next he was on the ground.

Nikki had charged him as if he were the quarterback in a championship game; then she'd run off. What had gotten into her?

The crowd around him had grown as people realized who he was. Everyone stared and a few pointed. Others had their cell phones out. No doubt wondering why a US congressman was sitting on their sidewalk. He stood up and brushed off his pants. "Everything's fine, folks." Then he walked over to the kid and held out a hand.

The young man got up and took his offered hand. "What is wrong with that woman? Does anybody know her name?"

Lucas smiled. "I'm sure she has a logical explanation."

Misty nodded. "He's right. Nikki would never assault some—"

"You do know her name. What's her last

name so I can tell the cops?"

Lucas put a hand on the young man. "Let's forget about that, shall we? She was trying to protect me, that's all."

"Protect you? She pushed you down harder than she did me. She's a menace and needs to be stopped. I want her arrested."

"There's no reason to do that. I'm really sorry she pushed you down, but as I said, she was only trying to protect me."

"She can't go around pushing people. This is America. We have laws against people assaulting other people for no reason."

Some of the people in the crowd nodded their heads in agreement.

Lucas needed to disperse the crowd before it turned into an angry mob who decided to go find Nikki and bring her to justice.

"You're right, this is America and she shouldn't have acted that way. I agree one hundred percent."

The crowd nodded.

He lowered his voice slightly, allowing his gaze to move from one person to another. "But this crowd reminds me of another crowd. A crowd where Jesus picked up a stone and told them to throw it if they were without sin. Not one took Him up on that offer."

They were listening.

"Now, I'm not Jesus, but I am asking for a little generosity of spirit for the woman. She really was trying to do the right thing. And just as all of us do from time to time, she didn't do it quite the right way."

People nodded and turned to go on their way.

Misty walked up. She leaned close and whispered, "You should have been a preacher, not a politician."

The young man glared at Lucas. "Those were nice words, but I still want her arrested."

As if on cue, a cruiser pulled up.

A moment later, Nikki was walking out of the alley and towards them.

Lucas hurried over to her. "Nikki, what happened? Are you OK?"

Her expression was grim. "I saw a man with a gun. He was aiming at you. Lucas, someone wants you dead."

10

Someone wants you dead.

Lucas heard Nikki's words but couldn't believe she was right.

"Did you hear me?"

"I heard you. I just . . . that doesn't make any sense . . . Are you sure?"

The policeman stepped out of his cruiser.

"Oh, great."

"Don't worry. I'll handle this."

"Let's get this over with." Nikki was resigned.

They walked back to the scene.

"Oh, you decided to come back, didja?" The young man turned to the officer. "I want her arrested. She assaulted me."

"I wasn't trying to assault you. I was trying to keep you from getting shot."

Lucas didn't let his concern show. He needed to diffuse this situation fast. But she could have been killed. What was she thinking when she ran after a man with a gun?

"I didn't see no man with no gun." The kid brushed the hair out of his face.

"Well, I did," Nikki countered.

"She's just making that up so she won't go to jail."

The police officer said nothing.

"If that was the case, then why did I come back?"

He glared at Nikki. "I don't know. Probably because you're crazy."

The officer looked at Lucas. "What about you, Congressman? Did you see a man with a gun?"

"My back was turned the other way. But if Ms. Kent says she saw a man with a gun, then she did."

"You need to contact the FBI." Nikki looked at the officer.

"FBI?" The officer raised his brows in inquiry.

"Lucas McMann is a US congressman. A threat to his life is nothing to minimize."

"If you want me to contact them, I'll be glad to do so." The officer turned to Lucas. "She's right. We don't want anything happening to you. Even if you didn't see the gun."

"What? You don't believe me?" Nikki asked.

"It's not that I don't believe you, ma'am,

but there's no proof."

"He's right," Lucas said.

"So, you don't believe me either." Her jaw tightened.

"I didn't say that."

"You didn't have to. Do whatever you all want." She walked away.

"Aren't you going to arrest her?" The young man asked, outraged.

"How about I pay for you and a friend to go out to dinner and you walk away with a good story? Just think, you quite possibly stopped a bullet intended for a congressman and the gunman ran away." Lucas kept his tone conciliatory as he pulled out his wallet and peeled off three one-hundred-dollar bills. "This will be enough to take your girl to a nice place and get a bottle of wine for your trouble."

The young man paused, looking at the cop.

The officer's face was noncommittal as he waited for a decision.

"OK." The young man snatched the bills, stuffed them in his pocket, and walked away. A moment later, he turned back. "You're a nice guy. I'll vote for you in the next election."

"Thanks." Lucas looked at the officer. "Are we done?"

"Unless you want me to contact the FBI."

"Not necessary. Thanks so much."

Nikki was halfway down the block.

Lucas hadn't meant to hurt her but he wanted to keep the stalking under wraps for now. *In case it's just me and I'm crazy.* He couldn't just let her walk out of his life feeling angry and betrayed. He jogged down the block. "Wait for me, Nikki." He caught up with her as she reached her car and put a hand on her shoulder.

She shrugged the hand away. "Go away, Lucas."

"I'm not going away, Nikki."

"That's OK. I am." She rummaged for her keys.

"I didn't say I didn't believe you. And for the record, I do. I was only saying there wasn't enough proof to get the FBI involved."

"You hired me to protect you, and then you fired me." She slid the key in the door lock. "I'm good at my job and you just allowed an audience to believe I am incompetent."

"First of all, I didn't hire you to protect me. I hired you to find out if I'm being stalked. And it seems you found that out today."

"A man pointed a gun at you today." She

117

gave him a serious look. "Aren't you concerned about that?"

"Of course I am. But there were three of us on that sidewalk. So technically, we can't be sure I was the target."

"Really. You think it could have been me or that kid? It was pretty obvious the officer didn't believe I saw anything."

"I believe you." He smiled. "I know what it's like not to be believed. I've been there. I've been living it for months. But we need to talk."

"You fired me. We have nothing to talk about."

"I wasn't exactly honest with you back there in the diner."

"Really? What a shock that is." She turned from him. "We've been down this road before too."

"Give me a chance, Nikki. I'll tell you everything this time. No secrets."

She glared at him for a time. Then she nodded. "Fine."

"Your sister's house."

She shook her head.

"You want to come to my house?"

She shook her head.

"Then the lake house it is. It's very private."

She nodded and looked at her watch. "I'll

meet you there at four."

"Let's make it six and I'll provide dinner."

"This is business, remember? Not a date."

"I know that."

"Six is fine." Her eyes scanned the area as if expecting to see another hit man. "Be careful. This is not a game, Lucas. Someone wants you dead."

11

Lucas stepped out of his car. The dogwood and mountain laurel were in full bloom. The front yard was sprinkled with pink and white blossoms. Of course, they weren't here to admire the scenery or to reminisce about their past.

An assassin in Maiden? It didn't seem possible. But he trusted Nikki with his life. The last email message flashed into his mind. *Someone will die if you repeat the same mistake twice.* What mistake? And who would die? The game had taken a nasty turn.

He popped the trunk on his mother's car and pulled out the picnic basket filled with fried chicken, sliced tomatoes, cheese and crackers, and some cupcakes. Did Nikki still love chocolate? Just because they had serious matters to discuss didn't mean they couldn't have a nice dinner as well. She'd be aggravated, but he didn't care. He had to break through that angry exterior she'd built up. He unlocked the door.

He'd set up the picnic supper outside. He moved through the house and onto the deck. Still a beautiful view. Even though they called it the lake house, it was more like a large pond. With the mountains and trees as a backdrop, the sun shimmered off the water. He took a deep breath, appreciating the beauty, the solitude, but mostly God.

As he laid out the food and the plates, he debated with himself.

Nikki had asked if she was hired again. A part of him wanted to say yes, because she was a very capable investigator. On the other hand, he didn't want to put her in danger. After the email and the gun incident, it seemed risky. Weighing the pros and cons, he decided he wouldn't ask her. He would simply tell her the truth and let her make her own decision.

He placed a small vase with flowers in the center of the table. Very nice. Candles would make it perfect. He headed into the kitchen to hunt for some.

Nikki sat at a table in Bethany's living room with her laptop, trying to focus on the computer screen. Lucas said he'd believed her, but now she understood why he'd started questioning himself and his sanity.

They had to talk, and she had to keep him safe. If he hired her back.

"I don't know why you won't let me help you." Not looking up from her tablet, Cassie whined as she sat cross-legged on the sofa. "Computers are kind of my thing."

"It's not necessary. I'm just browsing. I'm not looking for anything that important." Not exactly true. She wanted proof. If it was some sort of internet game, she should be able to find information about it. Games didn't usually involve guns and getaway vans.

"Yeah, so you say, but I know better. And it's also obvious you're not finding it. I really can help."

Nikki didn't want Cassie poking into Lucas's life for any reason. "Why is it obvious?"

"Because you keep sighing."

"I am not."

"Are too."

"That's because sitting at a computer is not my favorite thing to do. Unlike you kids today, I'd much rather be outside enjoying the spring weather." Nikki looked up from the screen. "Why don't you go outside? Do something. If nothing else, breathe some fresh air."

"Can't. Remember, I'm grounded."

"Oh, yes, I do remember that. Maybe next time, you'll remember not to leave the state without your parents' permission."

"Yeah, yeah. I hear you." A few minutes later, Cassie started laughing.

"What's so funny?"

She turned her tablet so Nikki could see it.

Nikki watched in horror as the events from the diner unfolded on the screen. And there was Lucas front and center. The next thing she saw was her pushing the kid down and then tackling Lucas before running across the street like a crazed woman. "Where did you find that?"

"Someone posted it on VidLife."

"That is awful." Nikki didn't know much about politics, but something like this could turn into a political nightmare. It made Lucas look foolish and weak. And he was neither. She wouldn't even think about what it made her look like.

"You didn't tell me you were playing football with Lucas McMann on the streets of Maiden." Cassie laughed and hit a button so the video could replay. "Or that he was even here."

"I had no idea he was here. We happened to run into each other at the diner."

"Happened to run into each other. What a

coincidence. Here comes my favorite part."
She watched for a moment, then yelled,
"Bam! Wanna see it again?"

"I do not." Nikki hoped it didn't go viral.

"Wait for it. Wait for it. Bam!" Cassie
looked up from her tablet. "You never did
tell me why he hired you."

"That's because it's private. Remember?"

"Does it have something to do with the
reason you're surfing the net?"

"What part of the word *private* don't you
understand?"

Cassie arched a brow. "A little sensitive,
aren't we?"

She didn't want to arouse Cassie's curiosity. Nikki forced herself to sound casual.
"Not at all. But my clients expect confiden-
tiality. Especially the politicians."

Cassie ran a finger across her lips. "It's in
the vault. I didn't even know you knew him
before yesterday."

"Well, he is from Maiden. He was a few
years ahead of me in high school."

"That would make him Mom's age."

She didn't want to talk about Lucas. But
if she got weird, that would set off alarms.
And who knew what Cassie would do?
"They're a few years older than him, I
think."

"I wonder why they never told me they

knew him." She changed the topic before Nikki could think of an answer. "How'd he find you down in Florida anyway?"

"Don't know. Didn't ask. But he's a congressman, so I guess it wouldn't have been too difficult. He probably has access to things us regular people don't. Do you know who posted that video?"

"No."

"Can you find out? And then ask them to take it down."

"Probably. But why would I ask them to take it down? I love it. It's hilarious."

"Because it's not very flattering to me or to him. It might hurt him during the election."

"Why exactly did you knock him down?"

Nikki stared at Cassie for a moment as an idea formed. Maybe, just maybe . . . "Hey, I need to take a closer look at that video."

"Why?"

Truth was always a good idea. "I knocked him down because I thought I saw a man with a gun. Nobody else saw it. But maybe he's in the video."

Cassie's eyes grew large, but she had no smart comeback comment. "I'll send it to your email address. Hold on." She hit a few buttons and then walked over to Nikki.

After Nikki opened the video, the two of

them watched several times. No gunman. "Oh well, it was a good idea even if it didn't pan out."

"True, but this is probably only a little part of the real video. I'll see if I can find out who posted it and ask to see the complete video."

"Good idea, Cassie. It has to be someone from Maiden, so you might even know them. If you find out, please have them take it down."

"Fine. I'll see what I can do."

Nikki checked her watch. "In the meantime, I have a meeting. Be back later."

"With Lucas?" Cassie's voice had taken on a teasing quality.

"He is my client, as you know."

"He's an awfully handsome client."

"Hadn't noticed."

Cassie was still laughing as Nikki walked out of the house.

She drove out to the lake house and forced her mind to stay in the present, not the past.

Lucas was in more trouble than he realized. He didn't seem to have taken the situation at the diner seriously. She had to make him understand that even if he had fired her.

She pulled into the drive.

The cabin was surrounded by trees, making it seem as if it was the only place for miles. She and Lucas had come here as teens — no disapproving parents, no one to tell them they were wrong for each other. But, in fact, the naysayers had been right. Life would have been a lot less complicated if she'd known how right they were, but then again, she wouldn't trade Cassie for anything in the world. Something good had come from their times up here.

Stop thinking about the past, girl. It's done and over with. Stay focused. Let's figure out what's going on so Lucas can get back to his life. And you can too.

She'd managed to muddle through and keep her head above water. Now God was obviously telling her it was time to leave the past where it belonged. Time to find the life God wanted for her. It was time to forgive Lucas — finally. Could she really do that? Closing her eyes, she laid her head on the steering wheel. She couldn't do that by herself.

But with God's help — maybe.

12

Lucas lifted the curtain.

Nikki sat in her car, not moving, an expression of pain on her beautiful face.

What a fool he'd been to listen to his father. Why hadn't he stood up for Nikki — for both of them? They could have made each other so happy. Life could have been so different if only . . . no use thinking about that. That was then and this was now.

Obviously, Nikki didn't have the same fondness for this place as he did. What was going on in her mind?

The lake house. The words had fallen out of his mouth so casually. Now that he'd had time to think about it, this probably wasn't the best place to have a talk. But remembering the good times could be healing for Nikki and for himself. They'd certainly had a lot of them up here. Sometimes just the two of them, but more often with their friends. Cookouts. Swimming. And just hanging around, before his father decided Nikki wasn't the right kind of girl for a Mc-Mann.

Before they'd given him an ultimatum right after graduation night — Nikki or his inheritance. Graduation night — the night Nikki had given in to him and given him her most precious gift. And he'd repaid it by turning his back on her instead of fighting for her. And today she hadn't hesitated to go chasing down a man with a gun to protect him. She certainly was the right kind of woman for any man. Why hadn't he seen that back then?

He'd learned to live with his choice, but now he had a chance to fix it. If nothing else, he needed her to know how sorry he was for the way things ended. If he had made her feel anything less than the truly amazing person she was then and still was now, he was even more sorry.

A part of him wanted to go to her, wrap her in his arms, and take away all the hurt. The hurt he'd caused. But that couldn't happen, so he'd settle for them being friends. If that was even possible.

Nikki opened the car door and stepped out. The sun shimmered on her blonde hair.

Lucas stood at the door and waved. "Hey, Nikki."

"I forgot how long of a drive it is out to here. I thought it was closer. Sorry I'm late."

"You call five minutes late?" He held the door open and motioned her in.

"Late is late. I happen to believe in punctuality."

"You'd do well in politics with that attitude. I brought us some supper."

"This is not a social engagement, Lucas."

"I know, but that doesn't mean we can't enjoy the view and some good food while we talk." He smiled. "Life is meant to be enjoyed."

"I enjoy my life just fine. It seems to me you should be more concerned about that gunman than how I live my life."

"I am and you'll probably be even more worried after —"

"After what?"

"After what I have to tell you." Lucas slid the deck door open and stood there. "But I'm sitting out here and eating a bite while we discuss the situation. I hope you'll join me." He sat down at the wooden patio table.

"Fine. You're the client."

He handed her a plate. "So what did you do with the rest of your day?"

"Let's cut the small talk." Sitting down, she picked up a chicken leg. After taking a bite, she nodded. "Not bad. I have two questions."

"Mama has a cook come in three days a week. Lucky for us, this was her day to work. I'm not much of a cook myself. Hot dogs and TV dinners are my usual." He filled his plate.

"You're supposed to ask me what my two questions are."

"Let's eat first and then talk."

"Are you intentionally trying to irritate me?"

"I'm trying to have a nice dinner."

She rolled her eyes. "Fine. I'll play along."

They chatted about nothing in particular as they ate. He put down his fork, and before he could change his mind, he said, "You don't know how much I regret the way I acted. If I could go back and change it, I would."

"But you can't." Her eyes misted over.

"And I can't tell you how sorry I am for the pain I caused you. I was young and stupid. I should never have listened to my father."

"You weren't in any position not to listen to him."

"You are the only woman I've ever fallen in love with."

"I doubt that very much. What about Victoria? And after her, between your good

131

looks and your money, I'm sure you had more than your fair share of women."

"You think I'm good looking."

"No comment."

He gazed into her emerald-green eyes. "Seriously, Nikki. I am so sorry for what happened." He reached across and touched her cheek. "You are my biggest regret."

It was her turn. She needed to say the words — to forgive him and move on. She wasn't sure she could breathe, let alone talk. Her heart softened for a moment. But she was the only woman he'd ever fallen in love with? Did he really think a few sweet words could undo the harm he'd done? How much he'd hurt her? And how that had led to so many bad decisions? No, she wouldn't let him off the hook that easily. How was she supposed to forgive him with so much pent-up anger? *Please help me, God.*

Lucas must think she was acting strangely.

Suddenly, the anger melted and she giggled. "Sorry."

He smiled back at her. "For what?"

"You gave me this wonderful heartfelt apology, and all I did was stuff some potato salad in my mouth."

"Well, it's very good potato salad." He picked up his fork. "Mmm. Good!"

"You're ridiculous."

"Me? You're the one with potato salad on your face."

She reached for her napkin.

"Just kidding."

"I . . . I . . ." *Say the words, Nikki. Be done with the past — with all the old hurt.* "I accept your apology." She hadn't actually said the word *forgiveness.* But it was implied.

"Thank you. That's not exactly forgiveness, but —"

"It's all I can do right now."

"And it's much more than I deserve. Remember the last time you were here?"

As if she could forget.

The two of them had met here one last time after both sets of parents made it clear the relationship wasn't to continue. And the only time their emotions had let them get too carried away.

"I'm not going down memory lane with you, Lucas." She stood up. "And I won't be part of whatever agenda you've decided on. I'm done. I came out here to discuss your problem. If that isn't what we will be talking about, I'm leaving."

"OK, OK. Let's talk."

She sat back down.

"Did you ever listen to the voice mail I left you?"

133

She nodded. "But it didn't really tell me much."

"I received an email the other night after I left your office. It was a picture of the two of us standing outside your office. And they sent a message with it. It said, 'Someone will die if you repeat the same mistake twice.' "

"You didn't think this was important enough for me to know?"

"Of course I did. I haven't had a chance to tell you. You didn't return my call and —"

"I think you could have found a way. We ate lunch together, remember?" She stopped. "Now I get it. That's why you fired me. You thought it might be too dangerous. You wanted to keep me safe."

"You make it sound like that's a bad thing."

"Just don't treat me like a helpless girl. I can take care of myself." She was touched by his concern.

"Yeah, Stanley and I both found that out."

"And don't forget it. So am I hired?"

"That's up to you, Nikki. But I really don't want to put you in harm's way. I would never forgive myself if you got hurt."

She ignored that comment. It probably came from guilt about what happened to his wife. "What do you think they were talking about? What mistake?"

"I have no idea. I thought it was about hiring you but that doesn't make sense. I've never hired you or any private investigator before, so . . ."

"So that can't be the mistake they're talking about. Did you make someone angry with something you did or didn't do?"

"Of course. No matter what politicians do, we make someone mad."

"Mad enough to kill you? You need to bring in the FBI or whoever it is that protects you people."

"The FBI didn't take me seriously."

"Maybe they'll take it more seriously now."

"As far as I can see, nothing's changed to make my safety any more of a priority than it was before. We still don't have any concrete proof. If the guy had taken a shot at us, that might make a difference."

She picked up a chocolate cupcake mounded high with chocolate frosting. "This looks great. Let's assume it wasn't a gun for a moment. Then why did the guy run when I chased him?" She took a bite. The chocolate swirled on her tongue. It had been a long time since she'd had homemade chocolate frosting.

"If he's part of the stalking, he wouldn't want to be caught, right? That could explain why he ran. Or it could be because you chased him."

"True, but if there is some sort of organized stalking going on, it's hard to imagine they ended up here in Maiden. After all, it's been months since you were here, and no one knew you were coming, right? They would have no reason to believe you would even be in Maiden."

"But they shouldn't have known I went to see you either. And someone showed up at your office. So what are you saying? You don't think the guy had a gun at all? It was just some guy taking my picture?"

Maybe it was the person responsible for the VidLife posting. One more thing she needed to tell Lucas about. "And was as harmless as the guy inside the diner. That's what I'm saying. It's possible I misjudged the situation."

"You? Misjudge? Is that even possible?" He grinned.

"It happens from time to time." She licked the frosting off her fingers. "On the other hand, if it was a gun, all bets are off."

"Well, was it a gun or not?"

She closed her eyes, thinking back to that afternoon. She opened them and stared into his blue eyes. "I can't be sure now, but I was positive it was a gun at the time."

"So what should I do? What's the plan? Should I resume my duties in DC with you following me as we originally planned? Or what?"

"I guess so, since I don't have a better idea. But if you have one, I'm all —"

A car backfired and Nikki fell backwards. A sharp pain in her arm suddenly spiked through her skin. She looked down at the spreading wet spot that turned one side of her shirt red.

"Nikki," Lucas yelled from somewhere — it sounded very far away.

Why was she lying on the deck?

Another explosion. Not a car backfiring — they were too far out to hear cars. A gunshot.

"Get down, Lucas. Someone's shooting at us."

Another bullet whizzed through the air.

The deck rattled as Lucas fell.

13

Dear God, not again.

Lucas dropped to the deck floor, then crawled around the table as more gunshots exploded.

Nikki was sprawled on the deck, her shirt bloody. Her eyes were closed. She wasn't moving and hadn't said anything since she'd yelled they were being shot at.

His mind flashed to Victoria lying on the floor of that convenience store. He blinked the memory away. Had to stay in the present. Had to help Nikki. When Lucas finally reached her, he put two fingers on her neck. A pulse — she still had a pulse. *Thank You, God.* He touched her cheek. "Nikki."

Her eyes fluttered open. "Someone's shooting at us."

"I know. You were shot. I need to stop the bleeding." He reached up to grab napkins off the table. Another shot exploded.

Her eyes fluttered shut once again. *Don't*

138

think about it. Just do what you have to do. He tore off his shirt and pressed it against her shoulder. "Nikki. Nikki. Wake up. Open your eyes. Please."

Her lids opened, but her gaze was unfocused. She moaned.

"Nikki, you've been shot."

"Kind of thought that." A weak smile.

"Lucas . . . house . . . need . . . to get . . . in the house." Her words burst out in short blasts.

"I'll carry you."

She grabbed his arm. "No. Can't . . . gotta . . . stay . . . down. Don't . . . give . . . target."

How could he move her? He didn't want to drag her. That might cause more damage, but they had to get off the deck. "Can you crawl?"

"Think so."

He helped her to her knees.

A path of blood marked her trail as she crawled towards the door.

Lucas hovered close behind her, shielding her from any more bullets.

Once they were in the house, Nikki sat back against the wall. Breathing hard. Sweat beaded on her forehead. So pale — just like Victoria.

He shook the thought away and knelt

139

beside her. "Let me —"

"Lock the doors. We can't let them get in." Her words came out between the gasps of pain. "And stay away from the windows."

"I need to —"

Her voice was adamant. "You need to make sure they can't get in the house."

He bolted the door they came through and then ran to the front door to bolt it. He'd not opened any windows, so they were as secure as they could be. Which wasn't much security at all.

Nikki still leaned against the wall when he came back, taking deep, slow breaths. Her eyes were closed.

He stared at her shirt, now covered in red. *Please, God, don't let her die.* He leaned down to her. "I'm right here, Nikki. The house is secure." Locked doors wouldn't stop them if they really wanted to get in. "Wake up. You can't go to sleep."

"Not asleep . . . trying to think. Did you call 911?" Her emerald-green eyes were cloudy with pain.

"Can't. There's no cell-phone signal out here. And the cabin doesn't have a landline."

She gave him a weak smile. "Well, I think we can assume I was right about the man with the gun."

"You're a tough one, huh? Making jokes

after getting shot."

"Don't feel tough. Feel tired. Arm hurts. Need to rest."

"I know it hurts, but you can't go to sleep right now." He touched her cheek. "I'll take care of you. I promise everything will be OK."

She stared at him with those beautiful green eyes, a lifetime of hurt and mistrust reflected back to him. Finally, she nodded. "I believe you."

Hearing those words meant more than he could say. He wouldn't let her down. "Let's get to the car before they make their way back here." He opened a drawer, pulling out several kitchen towels. He handed one to her.

Wincing, she pressed it against the wound. "Help me up." She leaned against him as they walked.

At the door, he stopped. "Maybe I should get the car and then drive as close as I can get to the door. That way, you don't have to run as far."

"No, let's go together."

"OK, let's do this." He opened the door and stepped out.

Gunshots split the quiet of the evening.

Lucas pushed Nikki back inside and

slammed the door. "Well, I guess that won't work."

"Must be two of them." Her face contorted in pain, and then her hand reached out to him as she crumpled to the floor.

His mind went blank. This couldn't be happening. He leaned over. Relief flowed through him when he found her pulse. She was still alive. He gathered her up and placed her on the couch. He checked her forehead, knowing it was a ridiculous thing to do. He relocked the front door. "Please, God. Keep her safe."

Nikki moaned.

"Nikki, can you hear me?"

She didn't respond.

Falling to his knees, he knelt beside Nikki. "Please, God, don't let her die too." He ran his finger down her cheek. Her skin was so pale and clammy — just as Victoria's had been.

The robbery had been a blur until the moment the gunman turned and aimed at Lucas. But he hadn't shot Lucas. It had been Victoria who fell to the floor.

His life had changed in a heartbeat.

Victoria's last heartbeat.

The papers had portrayed him as a hero. Some hero. He couldn't even save his wife.

And now Nikki was shot because of him.

The women he cared about always ended up hurt. Or dead. He closed his eyelids and prayed with all that was in him. He opened his eyes, leaning closer to Nikki.

Her breath was shallow, but she was still breathing. Nikki opened her eyes. "What happened?"

Tears filled his eyes. "You passed out and scared me to death."

"Sorry. How inconsiderate of me."

His hand brushed her cheek. "No, I'm the one who's sorry. For getting you in this mess. That's why I fired you."

"Listen to me." She grabbed hold of his arm. "Not your fault. It's my job. It's what I do."

"Then you should think about changing jobs."

"Yeah, maybe I should. And so should you. Apparently, someone doesn't like the way you're doing yours." She struggled to sit up. Gently, he helped her to a sitting position.

"I think you need to rest some more."

"We need to get out of here." She tried to stand, but swayed. Obviously, still woozy. She sat back down. "Maybe I'll rest for a minute. Need some water."

"How about some aspirin?"

"Bring me the bottle."

Lucas stopped in his old bedroom and found a T-shirt. As he was putting it on, he stared at the window. It might work. No — it would work. It had to. There weren't many other options for getting out of the house.

And he needed to get Nikki to the hospital. He grabbed a T-shirt for her and then hurried to the bathroom. His arms were full of first-aid things as he walked back into the living room.

Nikki's eyes were closed. Had she passed out again?

He breathed a sigh of relief as she opened them.

"Don't look at me as if I'm dead. It hardly even hurts."

"Yeah, right." He placed rubbing alcohol and bandages on the coffee table as he handed her the aspirin bottle. After she swallowed them, he sat down beside her. "Here, let me do this." He peeled off her blood-soaked shirt. Blood seeped from her arm, not her shoulder or chest. He looked for a corresponding bullet hole and found it. The bullet went through and through — wasn't that what they called it on those police television shows?

"Don't be looking at things you shouldn't." Nikki gave a weak smile.

He chuckled as he opened the rubbing alcohol. "Don't worry. That's the last thing on my mind. This will sting." He poured it on her arm.

She clenched her teeth. "Guess I'm not looking my best at the moment."

"You always look good." He took another towel and dabbed at her arm. "I don't think you're bleeding right now. Is that a good thing?"

"I don't know. I've never been shot before."

"Never been shot? What kind of private investigator are you?"

"The good kind that doesn't get shot."

He wrapped gauze around her arm and then used the surgical tape to keep it in place. "I'm so sorr—"

"It's not your fault. Stop apologizing." Their gazes met. "I mean it, Lucas. No matter what happens, you need to remember that. I made my own choices. Let's focus on getting out of this mess. You can be sorry later. Help me put on this T-shirt." She pulled the shirt down over her hips. "Sooner or later, they'll come in here to finish the job."

"I wonder why they haven't come in yet."

"Because they aren't sure if we have any weapons or not." She gave him a hopeful glance. "I don't suppose there are any guns here."

He shook his head.

"How can you not have guns at a cabin in the woods? A bear could pay a visit at any time."

"After my father died, Mama moved them into town. Guns make her feel safe."

"I can understand that. One would make me feel a lot safer right about now."

"Don't you have one?"

"I do, but it's in the car."

"Why?"

She gave him a sheepish look. "I had no need for it in here. I thought. Obviously, I was wrong."

"Aren't you the funny one?"

Their gazes met.

He saw the same sadness he felt when he thought about what might have been. He reached out and caressed her cheek. "I really am sorry."

"We need to be long gone before they decide to storm the house."

"I have an idea, but I'm not sure if it will work."

14

Nikki was glad Lucas had an idea, because she sure didn't. Between the pain and the blood loss, it was hard to think. But her mind was beginning to focus. She didn't think she'd die from the bullet wound. "So, what's your idea?"

"Come on, I'll show you." Lucas helped her to her feet.

Nikki stood up. "Good, no dizziness."

"Why don't I believe you?" Apparently, he didn't.

She took hold of his arm. "Well, not as much as before."

Lucas opened a door to a bedroom with two twin beds. "This room has windows facing the side. Hopefully, they aren't watching here. Maybe we could climb out and head into the woods that way."

Could she do that? She would have to. "At least it's large enough to climb through." Nikki looked out the window.

"That's quite a drop."

"That's because the cabin is built into the side of a mountain. I'll jump first and then I can catch you."

"I have a better idea. You go for help and I'll stay here."

"That's not happening." He shook his head. "I'm not leaving you."

"Oh yes, you are."

"I am not leaving you here with at least two shooters and no weapons to defend yourself. What kind of man do you think I am?"

She had to make him see reason. "I'll find a really good hiding place. When they come in and see the open window, they'll assume we both left through it. They'll either go after you or leave. Either way, I'll be fine. Chances are they won't even bother to look for me in the house."

"Not happening." His expression was adamant.

"If I go with you, I'll slow you down, Lucas. Please, listen to reason. You go get help — for me. It's the only thing to do."

"That's very noble, Nikki, but it won't happen. We're leaving together or we're not leaving. We can both hide. If your theory's right, it will work for both of us. They'll leave and we both live happily ever after."

"I suppose that could work."

"Your choice. We both leave or we both stay. Either way works for me."

She sighed. "When did you get so stubborn?"

"I'm used to getting my way."

"So I heard."

"What's your preference?"

"I don't like the idea of both of us being stuck here. One of us needs to get help and since I can't, I really wish you would —"

"I'm not leaving you this time. I did it once and it was the biggest mistake of my life. I'm not doing it again. I promised I would take care of you, and I will."

Why did he keep talking like that? It made it awfully hard to think clearly. "Then I guess we'll both go."

"Great." He smiled. "I'll get us a few supplies, and then we'll leave."

After he walked out, she slid to the floor. She just needed to rest for a minute, and then she'd be all right. She was still there when he walked in with a plastic grocery bag. "Just resting. I don't think I can do this. Please go without me."

"We both stay."

"OK, we'll both go." Using the wall as an anchor, she stood up.

He yanked the blanket off the bed, then

the sheets. He double knotted them.

"You really think that'll work?"

"I hope so." He looked around. "I need something heavy to tie it to."

She pointed. "The bed?"

He wrapped it around the footboard. After he'd tied the sheet to the bedpost, he pulled the bed to the window. "You're a lot lighter than me. So if it holds me, it should hold for you."

"I still think —"

"I know what you think, but we're staying together." He stared at her. "I mean it, Nikki. If I get out there and you don't come out, I'll walk to the front of the house."

"You wouldn't dare."

"Oh yes, I would." Their gazes locked. "Promise me, Nikki." His voice was soft.

She nodded.

"I'm not leaving until you say the words."

She rolled her eyes. "I promise I'll come out after you. Even though I think it's a mistake."

"Good enough. I trust you." After he unlocked the window, he tossed the grocery bag out. He turned back to her and grinned. "Say it one more time."

Her heart pitter-pattered as she remembered another time he'd said those words to her. Only then she'd told him she loved him. He'd hooted and hollered and made her say it over and over. In spite of the circumstances, her heart softened as unbidden tears filled her eyes. "I promise."

His returning smile was so sad that she wondered if his words had brought the same memory to his mind. "OK, time to get out of here." He tossed the sheet out then climbed through the window.

Nikki watched his progress as he shimmied down the makeshift ladder. The headboard scraped across the floor as his weight moved it, but the wall stopped the bed's sliding.

He was suspended midway to the ground. With a grin up at her, he let go of the sheets and landed in a heap. He stood up and brushed himself off.

She heaved a sigh of relief.

He gave her a thumbs-up and spoke quietly. "Your turn, Nikki."

In spite of giving her word, doubt crept in. He'd have a better chance without her. Surely he wouldn't really risk his life by walking to the front as he'd threatened. The look on his face gave her the answer. He would.

Besides, she'd given her word. She wouldn't break that trust. Grabbing hold of the blanket, she put one leg out the window.

Her arm throbbed as she eased through the opening. She moved one hand down the sheet rope and then the other. Tears streamed down her face as her injured arm screamed in protest. Sweat beaded up on her forehead from the pain. *I can do this. I can do this. I have to do this. Just a little further.*

"Go ahead and drop. I've got you. Trust me."

Trust Lucas McMann? That was something she never thought would happen. She let go.

He caught her. His arms cradled her. "I got you, Nikki." He set her upright and his hand brushed her hair.

Her knees buckled, and she slipped to the ground.

"Are you all right?"

"Just a little shaky." She leaned against the cabin, waiting for the excruciating pain to lessen. After a few deep breaths, she opened her eyes. A wet spot spread across the arm and side of the borrowed T-shirt. She was bleeding again.

A moment later, Lucas sat down beside her. He handed her a bottle of water and some more aspirin. "Here, take these. Hopefully, it will help with the pain. That probably hurt your arm."

"That's an understatement." She didn't think anything would help, but she popped the aspirin in her mouth and then took a sip of water. "I can't do this, Lucas. You need to go without me."

He smiled and touched her forehead. "Uh . . . no fever. I thought there would be since you'd have to be out of your mind to think I'd leave you sitting out here in the open alone."

Why wouldn't he listen? Why wouldn't he leave her like he had years ago? It hadn't seemed to bother him then. She looked at him, knowing the answer.

Because the spoiled rich boy had become a man — a good man — a godly man.

"There's no reason for both of us to die, Lucas. I'm only going to slow you down. Please, just go." Nikki leaned against the cabin.

His gaze met hers. "No one's dying today. It's not in God's plan."

They were in this together, whether Nikki liked it or not. He would protect her. He wouldn't let another woman he cared about die because of him. *God, give me the strength I need to do this.* "I'll let you rest for a minute and then we'll go."

"I want to get as far away from this cabin

as fast as we can. I don't need to rest. Let's go."

He took the bottle from her and placed it back into the bag. "Should we just walk across the field and into to the woods?"

"We can't be sure of their location or what they can see. So we need to keep a low profile. We scoot through the grass until we get to the trees. How far is it into town?"

"Twenty-five miles by the road, but a lot less through the woods."

"Still farther than I can go."

"There are other cabins closer. We could make a run to one of them but there's no guarantee anyone will be at them or that they'll have a working phone." He grabbed her hand. "Let's pray first."

"I haven't stopped praying since the shooting started."

After he finished, both of them moved to their stomachs. Side by side, they slithered through the grass. He could only hope they blended in with the environment. The approaching darkness helped keep them hidden as well.

Lucas looked over at Nikki. His heart skipped a beat.

She wasn't moving, her eyes were closed, and her head was on the ground.

He shook her gently. "Nikki."

Her eyes fluttered. "Sorry. Just tired." She started moving through the grass again. "These trees aren't getting any closer."

At the rate they were moving, they'd never get there.

A part of him wanted to pick up Nikki and run. But the other part knew it was better to stay hidden. "We'll get there — just like the turtle did."

"Slow and steady wins the race."

Gunshots and shattering glass exploded the silence.

"They're in the cabin." Lucas looked at her.

It would only take the bad guys a few minutes to figure out that he and Nikki were gone.

He'd hoped they'd be far away before the shooters realized their prey had slipped away.

Nikki nodded.

"We've got to get to the trees before they find out we're not in there. If they see us, they'll come after us. And they can outrun us." Lucas stood, leaned down, and scooped Nikki up into his arms. Still holding her, he ran towards the trees. Once they were in the trees, he put her down but kept an arm around her, half carrying her as they ran.

She leaned on him as they weaved their

way through the obstacle course. She was breathing hard and her face was pale and bathed in sweat. She'd never be able to walk to town.

"Let's take a rest break."

She nodded as she slid down the tree to a sitting position. Blood oozed down her arm.

He had to get her to the hospital. He peered through the trees towards the cabin. "I wonder what's happening in there."

"Nothing good, that's for sure. Let's go." She didn't look as if she could stand, let alone run. She used the tree as a brace to get up.

He started to help, but she shook her head in warning.

"We need to decide. Town or the nearest cabin?" he asked.

She closed her eyes. He wasn't sure if she was thinking or passed out again. Just when he was about to tap her, she opened her eyes. "I vote for town. I know it's further, but they'll expect us to go to the closest house. If they follow us, that's probably where they'll look."

"I agree."

"You go. I'll follow."

She was so pale he feared she might pass out again at any moment. As he turned, the men came around the corner of the cabin.

They stared into the woods, as if they were staring right at them. They weren't moving towards the woods. Yet.

Without a word, Lucas leaned forward and scooped her up in his arms. "Don't fight me, Nikki. They're staring at the woods. I can see them. They'll figure out we came this way." He jogged through the woods as he talked.

"I can —"

"No, you can't. You keep an eye out for them."

Her head dropped against his shoulder. A few moments later, she spoke. "I can't see them, Lucas. The trees are in the way."

"That's good. If you can't see them, that means they can't see us." He hoped that was the case. His breath was coming hard. It wasn't easy jogging through the woods carrying a woman. That wasn't a usual part of his exercise regimen at the gym.

"You need to put me down. I can walk."

"This is quicker, and besides, we don't have much further to go."

"We don't? We haven't gone anywhere near five miles yet. Unless I passed out again. Did I?"

"You didn't pass out, but I have an idea."

Her head dropped to his shoulder again.

Had she lost consciousness? "What's the idea?"

"There are some small caves in the mountain on the other side of the lake. We just have to get there and then we can hide."

She nestled in against him. Her breath warmed his neck. "OK."

"I promise to keep you safe, Nikki. I won't let them hurt you."

"OK. But whatever happens . . . not your fault." She sounded dazed, confused.

The darkness was coming fast, and that was good. It would provide more safety.

His foot hit something. He pitched forward but managed to drop to his knees instead of falling flat.

Nikki jerked. "What happened?"

"I tripped over something." He peered through the darkness. What if . . .

"I can walk."

"I have a better idea. Let's roll down the hill. Like we did when we were kids." He berated himself for such a stupid suggestion.

"Really? That's a great idea. That will be lots quicker."

Before he could say another word, she climbed out of his arms onto the ground, flattened out, and pushed off.

He did the same. When Lucas got to the

bottom, Nikki was sitting up.

"That might have been fun under other circumstances."

He helped her up and then put his arm out to support her.

The two of them walked up the hill, using the trees as cover.

Lucas couldn't hear anyone behind them. But that didn't mean they weren't there. If they were trained killers, they probably knew how to be quiet. A lot quieter than he and Nikki were being.

Nikki slipped from his arms and collapsed to the ground. "I'm OK. Just lost my footing."

Lucas scooped her up and struggled up the hill.

"I can walk."

"We have to keep moving." His arm and shoulder muscles burned with fatigue. It had been years since he'd even walked in these woods, or looked for the caves.

Scrapings and then someone cursing told him that they were much closer than he'd thought they would be. He leaned against the tree, whispering in Nikki's ear. "Quiet, they're not too far from us. But they can't see us. It's too dark." He eased them to the ground, still holding her across his lap.

As her breathing evened out, he realized

Nikki was asleep or passed out.

Looking around to get his bearings, he searched for something familiar, something to point the way. In the dark, he saw the shadow of a bent and gnarled tree. It had more branches, more tangles, but it was the same shape of the tree he recalled from years ago. Lucas picked up Nikki and then crept nearer. He waited in the darkness and moved to the right.

Nikki didn't wake up.

He dropped to his knees, still carrying her, and found the wild raspberry bushes. The thorns scratched as he reached through the bush and touched nothing.

He'd found the cave.

15

Nikki's eyes popped open, but darkness surrounded her. Panic bubbled up. Where was she? Where was Lucas? She was half lying, half sitting. Her back was propped up against something hard. A musty, earthy odor scented the air. Her hand reached out. She touched something. A shirt. "Lucas."

"Thank God, you're awake."

Just hearing his voice calmed her. She took a deep breath. "Where are we?"

"We're in the cave I told you about." His whispered voice tickled her ear. "They won't find us in here. We're safe."

"Are you sure?"

"The cave can't be easily seen even in the daytime. If you don't know it's here, you wouldn't be able to find it, especially not in the dark."

She nodded but he couldn't see her. She touched his arm. It felt warm. Safe. "Thank you."

"You have nothing to thank me for. This whole mess is my fault."

"How did you know about this cave?"

"It was one of my favorite places to hide when I was a kid. Suzie and I would play hide-and-seek. I always won."

Nikki smiled at the imagined scene. "Why are we whispering?"

"We don't want them to hear us."

"Oh, that makes sense." Her thinking was still fuzzy. In an effort to get more comfortable, Nikki twisted one way and then the other.

"You OK?"

"Just trying to get comfortable. I've got a rock jabbing my back."

"Well, that's not where I'm getting jabbed." He chuckled quietly. "Move over a bit. See if that helps."

She scooted towards him.

He put an arm around her shoulder and brought her even closer.

Her muscles tensed up.

"I'm just trying to get you comfortable, Nikki. It's damp in here. I thought you might be cold."

Her face warmed. "I know that." She leaned against him and closed her eyes. "How long will we stay here?"

"For a while. Until I think it's safe."

162

Would she ever feel safe again? She took several deep breaths.

"You OK?" His voice was filled with concern.

"It's just nerves. I've never had to hide in a cave after getting shot."

"It's a new experience for me as well. And one I hope I never have again."

"I'm with you. Talk to me." She leaned against him.

"About what?"

"Your life. What's it like being a congressman?"

"Like any job, there's good and bad. It can be very frustrating at times."

"Have you ever met the President?"

"Sure, we're in the same political party. I've had dinner with him. We've even golfed together a few times."

How weird was that? Most people would never meet the President of the United States, and yet Lucas thought it was no big deal. It was hard to imagine what his life was like.

"What about you? What's your job like?"

"Sort of like yours. Good and bad. I like when I can help people."

"Like Stanley's wife?"

"Yep. People come to me and I feel successful when I can do what they need. But lately . . . I don't know."

"But lately, what?"

"It's lost some of its appeal. I'd like something with less stress. Less . . . less ugliness. Something with more beauty." After she said the words, she felt foolish. "Never mind. It sounds stupid."

"It doesn't sound stupid to me. It sounds wonderful. So what would that look like in an ideal world?"

"I don't know. I like flowers. Flowers make people happy. Maybe I could live on a farm and grow tons of flowers."

"Sounds nice, Nikki."

"It would smell nice too. What's the best thing about your job?"

"That's a hard question. I'm not sure there's anything I like about it."

"Then why do you do it?"

"Good question. It was the plan we worked out. First, state government, then national, and one day, if everything went well, President."

"Is that your dream or your father's?"

"Another good question, Nikki. I'm not sure of the answer."

"Maybe you should be before you spend your life pursuing someone else's dream. What a waste that would be."

"I'll admit I used to want to be in politics

for the power to genuinely help people, but lately, that hasn't meant much. Power is an illusion. It's not real. Only God has real power. Everything can change in a moment, in a heartbeat. Just like tonight."

Even without being able to see him, she knew he was sad. "Are you thinking about your wife?"

"When she died, everything changed."

"I'm sorry."

"It's taken a while but I've come to grips with it."

"Did you have a good marriage?"

He was quiet for a moment. "We did, but it wasn't . . . I'm not sure how to explain it. We didn't have a traditional start to our marriage. Our parents decided we would be perfect for each other. And pushed us together." Another pause. "We didn't fall in love, but we grew to love each other. If that makes sense."

If she thought about her own life, that was true. "Nothing wrong with that. Sometimes strong emotions lead to big mistakes."

"Maybe, but there's something to be said for passion too."

She didn't want to think about that, especially with his arm around her. She changed the topic. "Why didn't you have any children?"

"I always wanted children, but Victoria refused to bring children into our loveless marriage. By the time the love was there, we found out she couldn't get pregnant. We thought about adoption, but never really followed through." He sounded sad again. "Guess I was too busy."

A stab of guilt penetrated straight into Nikki's heart. Lucas did have a child, but he would never know that. Cassie had a good life, and Nikki wasn't about to mess it up. "That's too bad." Her words sounded lame.

"What about you? Why no kids?"

Why had she brought up the subject of children? "Sort of like you. It wasn't that I didn't want children. It just never happened. In retrospect, I guess that was a good thing, considering the divorce."

"Why do you say that?"

"I don't think my ex would have been a good father. Besides, I sure wouldn't want to be tied to him for the rest of my life. Children deserve a happy, stable home." And that's exactly what Cassie had — and she would keep it.

"That's for sure."

She shivered.

"Cold?"

"A little."

Voices filtered into the cave.

Nikki tensed up. If those men found them, there was nothing they could do to protect themselves.

Lucas pulled her closer. "It's OK. They won't find us. "But just in case they do." Lucas took her hand and put something in it. A knife. Well, that was better than nothing.

The voices came near.

She laid her head on his shoulder.

His arm tightened around her. Lucas would keep her safe.

Good thing — she was too exhausted to do it for herself. Nestled in his arms, his breath warm on her neck, Nikki fought to stay awake, but her eyes drooped. Against all common sense, she felt safe.

Even though the gunmen were out there looking for them. Even though they were hiding in a cave.

Lucas promised he would take care of her.

And she believed him.

Nikki's breathing grew even. That had to be a good thing.

He whispered her name.

No response. She must have fallen asleep.

Lucas thought about Nikki on a farm, growing flowers. It sounded like a wonderful idea. If they got out of here, he'd help her make her dream come true. She deserved a happy ending.

It had been a while since he'd heard the voices. Had they given up and left? Or were they out there, still searching for them?

He couldn't stay here all night. He hated leaving Nikki, but he needed to get her to a hospital. He couldn't believe she wasn't in shock.

Maybe she was.

Lucas slowly moved his arm out from under her neck. She stirred a bit but didn't wake up. He crawled towards the cave entrance and stopped. No voices, but that didn't mean they weren't out there, doing exactly what he was doing.

Waiting and listening.

Leaves rustled and then footsteps crept across hard-packed dirt. They were still out there. Or maybe it was an animal? Bears roamed this area.

He wasn't sure which he'd rather face. The bear or the gunmen.

A bump and then an uttered oath. Human. The most merciless hunter in the animal kingdom. From the sounds, the man had to be almost directly in front of the cave opening.

"I can't believe this," a man's voice whispered.

"They have to be here."

"We don't know that. We have no idea when they got out of that house. I say we go and try again tomorrow."

"We've already struck out twice. I'm not trying a third time. I'm not leaving until this is finished. I want my money."

So someone had hired them to kill him. If they moved the brush away, they would see the entrance — and him.

Lucas backtracked and found the knife. He shuddered at the thought of using it on a person, but he'd do what he had to do to protect Nikki. He crawled back to the entrance.

They were still there, though they weren't talking. Their breathing gave them away.

Did they have any idea they were by the cave where Nikki and Lucas were hiding? They might. They could be calling in reinforcements. At any moment, they could find them.

He had to get them away from the cave — away from Nikki. He crawled closer to the entryway and waited. After a moment, he quietly pushed leaves aside.

They had to move away from this cave. Away from Nikki.

And if that meant being the bait, then so be it.

Left or right? He had no idea where the men were. He crawled out of the cave and turned to his right until he came to a tree. He moved behind the trunk to keep hidden for a bit, stood up, and moved onward, away from Nikki. Then he started running, making as much noise as possible, thinking they would hear him and follow. A moment later, his hope turned into reality.

"This way. I hear something."

Now if he could keep them from catching him. He sprinted down the hill away from Nikki and the cave. Maybe he could make it to his car. The keys were still in it. Suddenly, the trees were gone and the cabin was in front of him. He sprinted up the hill, past the cabin, and towards his car. As he neared it, his great plan evaporated.

All the tires on his car and Nikki's were flat.

He ran past the cars and jumped across the drainage ditch. He considered going back into the woods. The trees could help to protect him, but he could move much quicker on the road. He had to keep moving. He was a fast runner, but they might be faster.

And they were the ones with the guns.

A pair of headlights shone as he rounded a curve. Lucas stood in the road and raised his hands, praying the driver wouldn't run him over. The car slowed. He grabbed the passenger door, opened it, and jumped in.

The woman looked terrified.

"Go. Someone's chasing me. We need to get out of here." Something in his voice must have told her he was speaking the truth.

The car surged down the road.

Lucas looked at the rearview mirror.

Two men stood on the road, staring at them.

"Thank you." Lucas looked at the woman. "Do you have a cell phone? I need to call the police."

16

Lights — too bright — and people — lots of people — surrounded her. "I . . . what's . . . where . . ." Nikki opened her eyes. She squinted at Lucas, whose hand surrounded hers. His grip was strong and warm. His soft blue eyes were filled with concern. As she stared at him, the craziness around her receded.

He'd promised to take care of her and he had.

"It's OK, Nikki. You're at the hospital. Everything will be fine."

Someone squeezed her other hand.

Bethany walked beside her with tears rolling down her cheeks.

"Bethany . . ."

Bethany smiled through her tears. "Don't worry, Nikki. The doctor says you'll be fine. Ray is scrubbing in. He'll be with you the whole time."

"Ray?"

"He'll take care of you. I love you, sweetie." Her sister's hand fell from hers.

Nikki nodded and then looked back at Lucas. Cave — darkness. Being shot — men chasing them. Lucas carrying her through the woods. Lucas holding her in that dark, scary cave. Dear, sweet Lucas. "How'd I get here?" she mumbled through the air mask someone had put on her.

"You passed out while we were in the cave, so I hitched into town to get help."

"The men — did they catch them?"

Lucas shook his head, but before he could answer, a woman in scrubs walked up beside him. "I'm Dr. Vines, Ms. Kent. We're taking you into surgery to make sure the bullet is gone and to repair any damage."

Lucas's hand slipped from hers and she suddenly felt alone.

The doctor smiled and patted her arm. "Don't worry, Ms. Kent. We'll take good care of you."

Another doctor walked up. He lowered his facemask. Ray. "Don't worry, Nikki. I'll be right here. Take a few deep breaths and count backwards from a hundred."

She wished everyone would stop telling her not to worry. It was making her worried. "One hundred . . . ninety-nine . . . ninety . . ."

■ ■ ■ ■

A nurse came running into Nikki's hospital room.

"I want to go home."

The nurse glared at her. She pointed at the button Nikki held in her hand. "That is called an emergency button. Not a whining-and-complaining button."

"Aren't you a funny one?"

The nurse cracked a smile. "I do my best."

"I hate this place." Two days in the hospital was more than enough time to recuperate from her bullet wound. It was barely more than a flesh wound.

"We do that on purpose so you'll want to get better."

"I'm all better. I want to go home."

"With Congressman McMann breathing down our neck, you are our star patient. You're not going anywhere until you're a hundred percent."

"When will that be?"

"The doctor said he'd check on you this evening, but you probably aren't going home until tomorrow morning." The nurse put her hands on her hips. "If then."

"I am not going to be here for a few more days. I feel fine."

174

"I can attest to that," Cassie said from the recliner, tablet in her hands. "A sick person wouldn't have the energy to complain this much."

"Isn't that the truth?" The nurse looked back at Nikki. "Your body has been through trauma, Nikki. Give yourself time to heal."

"Do I have a choice?"

"Not really. Doctor's orders." She gave a little wave and walked out of the room.

The door opened back up.

A little gray-haired lady walked in.

More than a little shocked, Nikki stared. She hadn't seen her in sixteen years.

The woman walked up to her. "Ms. Kent, I'm Isabella McMann, Lucas's mother."

"I know who you are." Nikki didn't have the energy to play games. "I just never expected . . . what are you doing here?"

"I came to make sure you're all right. I was worried after Lucas told me about your ordeal."

Why would the woman worry about her?

Mrs. McMann's gaze moved to Cassie.

Nikki didn't want Cassie near any of the McManns.

The woman turned back to Nikki. "Lucas will be along in a few minutes, but I had something I wanted to say to you. In private."

"I can take a hint." Cassie stood up.

It was almost as if the woman was warning Nikki.

"Cassie, you need to get back to school anyway."

The high school was only a block away from the hospital and Cassie had walked over during her lunch.

"But I have a good excuse not to go. The teachers won't mind." She smiled at Mrs. McMann. "But that's OK. I'm going."

"Stop back after school and bring me something good to eat. This place doesn't know the meaning of *seasoning*." Nikki made a half-hearted motion towards Cassie. "This is my niece."

"I know exactly who she is," Mrs. McMann said, her articulation clear and crisp.

Nikki stared. Did the woman really know who Cassie was? That was impossible.

"I've heard her sing several times at different functions. You have the voice of an angel, my dear."

"Thanks, Mrs. McMann. Gotta go. I don't want to upset my auntie by not going to school." Cassie walked out of the room.

Nikki found it difficult to meet the older woman's gaze.

"I am so sorry about all of this. It must have been perfectly horrible. I'm so glad you survived."

"Me too."

"I wanted to come see you before Lucas arrives." Mrs. McMann cleared her throat and then met her gaze head-on. "I owe you an apology."

"It's not your fault. You didn't shoot me, and I'm pretty sure you didn't hire them to shoot Lucas. Unless you have a confession you'd like to make."

Mrs. McMann laughed. "I can assure you I had nothing to do with that. That's not what I'm apologizing for."

Nikki's heartbeat ramped up. "Oh."

"I came to apologize for what my husband and I did all those years ago. For paying your parents to keep you apart. I hope you'll forgive me."

Anger raised its ugly head. Several responses came to mind. None of them had anything to do with forgiveness, but Nikki was tired of her anger, her bitterness. Tired of letting other people's actions control her emotions. Nikki stared at the woman who had changed the course of her life without one bit of concern. She had a choice. Stay stuck in the past. Or forgive. *God, help me do the right thing.* Nikki took a deep breath. "That was all a long time ago, Mrs. McMann." A lifetime ago.

"Call me Isabella."

"As I said, no apology is necessary, Isabella."

"An apology is exactly what is needed. Because it happened a long time ago doesn't mean it doesn't matter. I could blame it all on my husband." The woman sighed. "But the truth is I agreed with him. I'm sorry for any pain our actions might have caused you."

It hadn't just been the McManns and her own parents. It was time she accepted some of the responsibility for her life choices as well. After all, she'd gone along with them. "Thank you so much, Isabella." Nikki meant the words.

"From what Lucas tells me, you are quite the remarkable woman."

"I don't know about that. He was the one who saved me."

"My son is a good man."

"I can't argue that point. It was very nice of you to come. I accept your apology, even though it wasn't necessary."

The woman nodded. "That is very kind of you. Thank you for helping Lucas. That was so incredibly gracious of you, considering everything." She turned to leave but then turned back to Nikki. "Lucas is lucky to count you among his friends."

Had she and Lucas renewed their friendship in the middle of the chaos they'd shared? She wouldn't have thought it possible a week ago, but Isabella might be right. "Thank you for coming, Isabella."

"You're welcome." Mrs. McMann turned back. "Your . . . niece is lovely. If she ever needs anything, you be sure to let me know. I'll be glad to help her in any way I can." Mrs. McMann turned and left the room.

The woman couldn't possibly know that Cassie was her granddaughter.

Nikki lay back against the pillow, thinking about Isabella's apology. The situation seemed so much clearer. After all the years of anger and bitterness, she could see her own part in it. How she'd gone along with the plan. At any time, she could have gone to Lucas. Told him she was pregnant. For years, she'd been angry because he'd abandoned her. But he hadn't done any such thing. She hadn't given him the chance to do the right thing.

A sense of calm — of peace — enveloped her. Her Christian mentor was right. Forgiveness wasn't about letting the other person off the hook — it was about giving up the anger. It wasn't about the person she forgave. It was about her. Letting go of that anger gave her back the freedom to be herself. She closed her eyes, savoring the feeling. *Is this what forgiveness feels like?* Nikki smiled. She liked the feeling. She was still basking in it when the door opened.

Lucas walked into Nikki's hospital room, carrying a huge bouquet of red roses.

Her eyes were closed, but she looked at peace. Almost angelic. She definitely looked better than the last time he'd seen her.

God was so good to keep her safe.

She opened her eyes. "My goodness. Did you leave any at the flower shop for anyone else to buy?"

"Not a one." He placed the vase on her tray table. "And you deserve every one and more."

"They're beautiful, Lucas."

"Not as beautiful as you." The doctors had assured him there'd been no major damage from the bullet. They expected a full recovery. "How are you?"

"I'm alive and feeling pretty grateful about that."

"I'm very grateful for that as well."

"That you're alive?"

"Very funny." Did she have any idea what an amazing woman she was? Strong. Brave. And a good sense of humor. She'd be so easy to love. "No, I'm very glad that you're

180

alive." He stepped closer. His hand reached out to caress her cheek, but Nikki grabbed it and moved it away. Her action startled him back to reality. Nikki would be easy to love, but he wasn't the one to do it.

She smiled at him. "Oh, well, thanks for that. And for the flowers. They're beautiful, but it wasn't necessary."

"You're very welcome. I would have been here sooner, but it was family only in the ICU. Can you believe they wouldn't make an exception even for me?"

"Must be losing some of your influence." She smiled. "By the way, your mother was here a little while ago."

"Really?"

"She apologized for paying my parents to keep us apart."

He sat down in the chair by her bed. "I can't believe that. We haven't even discussed it in years."

"You could've knocked me over with a feather. If I'd been standing and not stuck in this bed." Nikki hit a button on the side of her hospital bed. It moved her to a sitting position.

"I hope it didn't upset you too much."

"Not in the least. She was quite gracious. Your mother is a very classy lady."

"It sounds as if you were nicer to her than

to me when I apologized."

"Maybe so. But I'll be glad to rectify that. I'm over it, Lucas. Over all of it. You are more than forgiven."

"Ah, shucks." He smiled, wishing it were true. "You're just saying that because I saved your life."

"It has nothing to do with that. The past is the past and I'm looking forward to the future. At least I will be as soon as we catch the bad guys. How's that going?"

"Not so good." He could see the peace in her eyes. All the anger was gone. She even looked younger. For a moment he was whisked back to the past — their past. All those feelings bubbled up. "You really forgive me?"

"Actually, I don't."

"But you just s—"

"I don't forgive you, because I came to the realization you did nothing that needed to be forgiven."

His gaze held questions.

"Your parents, yes. My parents, yes. Maybe even a little bit me. But you. You were as much of a victim as I was. Maybe more. You had no idea of the deal between our parents, but I did."

"I don't know what to say. That's wonderful, Nikki."

Her green eyes sparkled. "It was probably the best thing for everyone involved anyway. Our parents were probably right even if they did it in the wrong way. The truth is we were both way too young to be involved in that intense of a relationship."

"Oh, you remember that, do you?"

Her face turned rosy pink.

"Behave." She gave him a playful tap on his arm and then her expression turned serious. Her eyes probed his. "How are you, Lucas?"

"I didn't get shot. I'm fine."

"I don't think you are." Her voice was quiet.

"What's that mean?"

"It means you need to give yourself a break."

"I have no idea what you're talking about."

"Oh yes, you do."

Their gazes met. It was as if she could see deep inside where all his secrets were. "You getting shot was my fault. They were after me, not you."

"I'm not talking about me. I'm talking about Victoria."

Pain coursed through his heart. "That was my fault. And this is my fault. If I hadn't contacted —"

"It's not true, Lucas. You are not God.

You don't get to control everything. Everything bad that happens in this world is not your fault."

He couldn't speak.

"I forgive you. God forgives you. Isn't it about time you forgive yourself?"

"I don't want to talk about this." He stared at her and sat down. "But I do want to talk with you."

"About what?"

"Flower farms."

Her eyes widened. "Flower farms? Why on earth would you want to talk about that?"

"In the cave, you said that you would love to live on one. I want to make that happen."

"I don't understand."

"What's not to understand? You want to live on a flower farm and I want to buy you a flower farm. When you're better, we'll start hunting —"

"You can't buy me a flower farm."

"Of course I can. End of discussion. Did I tell you I have bodyguards around the clock?"

"We're not done discussing flower farms."

"They follow me around like puppies."

"How many? I would have thought you rated at least three." She grinned.

"Three it is, one for each eight-hour shift.

I've arranged for private security for you when you get out. Until they find out who's behind this."

"I don't need any security. You're the target."

"You're probably right, but I'm not taking any chances."

"I don't need security, Lucas. And that's the final word, so un-arrange it. Please."

Didn't she understand he wanted to keep her safe? He wanted . . . "That's not a good idea. Someone shot you, Nikki."

"But the bullet was meant for you. You're the one who needs security, not me." Lucas reached for her hand, but she picked up her glass of water. "But —"

"Lucas. Lucas. Lucas," a loud voice yelled from the other side of the door. "They won't let me in."

"Apparently, my security's doing their job." He held up a finger. As Lucas opened the door, a woman threw herself into his arms. "Are you all right? I can't believe you didn't call me. I had to see it on the news. I was worried to death."

"As you can see, I'm perfectly fine." He moved out of her embrace and turned towards Nikki. "This is my assistant, Elizabeth Roar. And the beautiful woman in the bed is my dear old friend, Nikki Kent."

"Who are you calling old, mister?"

"So true. I am older than you."

Still holding Lucas by the arm, Elizabeth's gaze landed on Nikki. "It must have been a harrowing experience." She turned back to Lucas. "It's lucky Lucas was with you. He's quite the hero, you know. The TV reporters say he ran through the woods as the men chased him just to get help for you."

"I didn't know that. Why didn't you tell me that, Lucas?"

"The TV exaggerated. I'm not the hero — you are." He turned back to Elizabeth, not quite sure why she'd come. A phone call would have been more than enough. "The FBI finally believes me."

Elizabeth rolled her eyes. "It's about time. I'll make sure someone gets fired over this."

"That's not necessary."

"Well, someone has to pay."

"Elizabeth's the only one who believed me from the start."

"I must admit you seemed rather paranoid when you first walked into my office." Nikki adjusted her pillow. "I wasn't quite sure myself."

He laughed. "I knew you didn't believe me."

"True, but I was willing to do my best to discover the truth."

Elizabeth moved closer, still holding his arm.

He took a step away.

"I knew Lucas couldn't make up such a thing." She patted Lucas's arm. "So, when are you coming back home? I . . . we miss you."

"I'm not exactly sure, but I'm sure you can hold down the fort until I get back." He extricated himself from Elizabeth and moved over to Nikki's bedside. "Elizabeth is a wonderful assistant. I wouldn't be half the congressman without her."

"Flattery will get you anywhere." Nikki laughed.

"I have to admit I was a bit miffed when you missed your appointment with Senator Callahan, but this will make for an even bigger and better story."

Lucas shook his head. "I don't want to use it that way."

"We'll talk about it later, Lucas." Elizabeth eyed Nikki. "I guess I wasn't really needed here. As usual, I overreacted. I guess I'll fly back to DC."

"Of course you're very needed. I appreciate you coming. As you can see, I'm fine."

Elizabeth smiled. "Well, I guess I'll go. Of course, I'm so exhausted, but I can sleep in tomorrow. The boss is away."

"No need to go home tonight. You can stay the night at my mother's house and leave tomorrow. Do you know how to get to Mother's?"

"I have the address. And my rental has a GPS. I'll find it."

"Lucas, you don't need to stay here. Go ahead and take Elizabeth to your house."

"We haven't finished our conversation."

Elizabeth smiled. "That sound like a great idea, Lucas. Then you can tell me every little detail. I'm sure we can use this whole situation to work for us. I'll set up some interviews for next week. We need to make a big splash with this. The voters will love you even more than they already do. Watch out, senators. Here we come."

Lucas looked at Nikki and then back at Elizabeth. "I already told you this is not about politics."

17

"Not about politics. Of course it is. You're all about the politics." Elizabeth's head tilted back as she laughed.

"I told you so, Lucas. If it's about you, then it's about politics," Nikki chimed in.

"Not this time. I am not going to exploit what happened to you, Nikki, for political gain."

"We shall see." Elizabeth smiled.

Did Lucas have any idea how much the woman cared for him? It was so obvious. Elizabeth only had eyes for Lucas. And the way she clutched his arm as if she owned him.

The surge of jealousy surprised her. Nikki pushed it away. She had no right to be jealous of Lucas. Even if the last few days had brought back some of those long-ago feelings, they couldn't be together. Ever.

Lucas shook his head, but his eyes twinkled. "It's not true. Apparently, no one knows the real me. I'd be just as happy on a flower farm as in DC." His gaze met Nikki's.

Nikki's heart skipped a beat.

"Don't be ridiculous, Lucas. You can't be President and live on a flower farm."

"Who said I wanted to be President?"

"You did. Many times." Elizabeth's voice was adamant.

"Maybe it's time for a change." Lucas took Elizabeth's hand off his arm and moved to Nikki's bedside. "Enough about politics. And I'm not going anywhere at the moment. Nikki got shot because of me. The least I can do is keep her company while she's recuperating. Elizabeth, you are more than capable of finding your way to my house without me."

Disappointment crossed Elizabeth's face, but only for a moment. Then she brightened up. "You are absolutely right. I'm very capable of taking care of myself." The way she said it made it sound as if Nikki wasn't capable of the same.

"Go with her, Lucas. I'm very tired. I really need to take a nap."

"OK, but I'll be back later to check on you. And we can talk some more about flower farms."

Elizabeth moved closer to Lucas, a smug smile on her face. "Please stay. I can find

190

my way."

"Elizabeth is probably right. You need to get back to work and get busy with those interviews. Gotta strike while the iron is hot, as they say."

A flicker of hurt grazed his expression, but he smiled. "I'll be back later to check on you. You aren't getting rid of me that easy."

"It's not necessary."

"Necessary or not, I'll be back." He turned to Elizabeth. "Let's go."

"If you don't mind, can you get your car and pick me up at the entryway of the hospital?" Elizabeth asked. "I'm so tired I don't think it would be safe for me to drive. But I do want to talk with Nikki for a moment to make sure there's nothing else we can do for her."

"I can do that." He left.

Elizabeth touched the flowers. "These are beautiful. I assume they're from Lucas."

Nikki nodded.

Elizabeth walked over to her bed. "Lucas is a stand-up guy and it's obvious he's feeling guilty about you getting shot. After all he's been through with his wife and now this fiasco, I would hate to see him mistake guilt for" — She paused as if searching for the right words — "well, for something more than it is."

Fiasco? Her getting shot was more than a fiasco. But she understood what Elizabeth was hinting at. "There is nothing between us."

Elizabeth nodded. "How is it that the two of you were up at the cabin alone?" She fluffed a hand at Nikki. "Oh, never mind. Lucas's love life is not my business. But I'd hate to see him hurt."

"I don't know anything about his love life. I think he has bigger issues at the moment. Like finding out who's trying to killing him."

"So true. So true. Just remember his real life is politics. His career means everything to him." Elizabeth gave a small wave. "Tootles."

After she'd gone, Nikki lay back down on the pillow. She was exhausted. Tears pushed against her eyelids. "This is ridiculous," she mumbled as tears slid down her cheeks. Why was she even crying? She didn't feel that way about Lucas. And Elizabeth was right — Lucas belonged in Washington, not on a flower farm.

Elizabeth was the perfect woman for Lucas. Sophisticated. Beautiful. Intelligent. That outfit she had on probably cost more than Nikki's yearly clothing budget. Elizabeth traveled in his circles, understood politics, and it was obvious she cared about Lucas.

Nikki wiped away the tears dripping down her cheeks.

Elizabeth was the type of woman to help Lucas get to the White House.

How had this happened? When had this happened? She'd opened her heart to Lucas once again. But it was time to close it, put a lock on it. They could never have a future together.

The door opened, but Nikki kept her eyes closed, hoping they would go away.

"What's wrong, Auntie?" Cassie's voice was filled with concern.

Nikki opened her eyes and attempted a smile. "Nothing. Probably feeling the after-effects of the anesthesia. They said some people get a little weepy."

Cassie walked to her bedside and hugged her as best she could through the wires and tubes. "Of course that's it. It couldn't have anything to do with being shot. You don't have to act that tough all the time, Auntie."

Nikki patted Cassie with her good arm. "You're right. Why are you back? It's not time for school to be out yet."

"My principal said it was OK for me to leave, so I did. Don't get mad. I was worried about you."

"That's sweet."

"That's me." Cassie grinned. "I met the senator's assistant as I was coming in. You'd think the great man could come himself rather than send his assistant. Since you got shot because of him. How rude."

Nikki pointed at the flowers. "He was here and it wasn't his fault I got shot."

"That's a matter of opinion. So, do they know who shot you?"

"Not yet, but the FBI is investigating."

"Well, it makes me really mad." Cassie pulled the chair closer to her bed. She laid her head on the mattress near Nikki. "I was so scared."

More tears leaked from Nikki's eyes as she caressed her daugh— her niece's hair. "I'm fine, Cassie. All's well that ends well, as they say."

Cassie sat back up. "I know, Auntie. But with the job you have, you might not be all right the next time. I don't want that to happen."

"It won't. And besides, it wasn't me they were aiming at. I just happen to be the one the bullet found."

"See, it was his fault."

The nurse opened the door. "Hey, your guard's gone."

"That's because he wasn't mine."

"That makes sense. Time for a walk. Let's get you up and moving." She unplugged some of the wires. "OK, you can sit up." Then she took the blood-pressure cuff off.

"It feels good to have that thing off."

"Good news. You've graduated to only having it taken every few hours."

"Lovely."

"I thought you'd like that. Alrighty, you can stand up. Lean on my arm while you get up."

Once Nikki was standing, the nurse turned to Cassie. "She's all yours. She needs to at least walk down to the end of the hall and back. Gotta keep her moving. We don't want her to get blood clots. They're nasty little things."

"Yes, ma'am. Let's go, Auntie."

Nikki held on to Cassie's arm. "I don't like feeling like an invalid."

"Then stop getting shot."

"I'll remember that next time."

"Next time? See, your job is too dangerous, and you know it."

They walked down the hall, one slow step at a time.

"Hey, did you find anything out about that video?"

"I found the person who took it and he sent me the complete video. I didn't see anyone with a gun. The camera must have been at the wrong angle."

"Let's stop a minute." Nikki couldn't believe she was winded already. She leaned against the wall. "Thanks for trying. Did you talk him into taking down the video?"

"Uh . . . not exactly."

Oh well . . . After a moment, she straightened up.

They proceeded down the hall.

"I don't understand why you want a job where people shoot you."

"That's a good question, my sweet niece." A flower farm didn't seem like such a bad idea at the moment.

"Maybe it's time you change jobs."

"Maybe it is. How'd you get so wise, young one?"

Cassie grinned. "Don't know. Guess I was born that way."

"That woman is in love with you," Lucas's mother whispered even though they were alone in the kitchen.

Elizabeth was upstairs getting settled in.

Lucas laughed. "Don't be ridiculous, Mama. I admit she worries about me too much. But that's a lot different than being in love with me. She's a good friend. That's all. She was a good friend to Victoria as well."

"I'll just bet she was. She came here as soon as she'd heard about the shooting. I call that more than a good friend." His mother shook her head.

"I call it worry and a very good friend."

"It's been more than a year since Victoria died. It's not too soon to be thinking about a new relationship. She might be the right woman."

"Yeah, like you did after Dad died."

"That's different. I was an old lady when your daddy died, but you're a young, healthy man who needs . . . well, let's just say, companionship. And the truth is you could do worse than Elizabeth."

"I'm not in the market for a wife." But as he said those words, he knew that wasn't exactly true. It would be nice to share his life with someone, but it wasn't in the cards. He wouldn't take that chance again, and besides, Nikki had his heart, as she always had. There was no substitute for her. "And if I were in the market, it wouldn't be Elizabeth."

"Then who would it be?" Those wise eyes of hers pierced through his skin, staring straight into his heart.

"Mama . . . don't go there."

"I've learned a few things in the many years I've been on this earth. And one of those is that we have a tendency to look at the past through rose-colored glasses. The reality was never as good as our memories."

He shook his head. He couldn't hide a thing from his mother. "Leave it alone, Mama."

"I'm just saying." His mother held up her hands in surrender. "When is Elizabeth leaving?"

"Tomorrow. She's exhausted. Was it all right that I invited her to stay?"

"Of course. It's your house too. Even if you do stay in the guesthouse. I don't know why you won't stay in the main house with me."

"To remind myself that I'm an adult. Living with my mother at this age is shameful."

She giggled. "It's not shameful. It's what a good son does. My monthly tea is on Saturday. I'm wondering if I should postpone it in light of the events of the past few days."

"I don't think it's necessary. If you're feeling uncomfortable, we can hire some private security."

"I'll let that up to you. Just thinking about such things gives me the heebie-jeebies."

"Then have your tea party. I'll make sure

everyone is safe."

"Maybe Elizabeth would like to stay a few more days so she can attend the tea."

"Are you trying to be a matchmaker, Mama?"

"Absolutely not!" She winked. "Besides, I know better than to get involved in your love life. I learned my lesson."

"Good."

"Do you forgive me, Lucas?" Her eyes turned serious. "I know we were wrong to interfere. But you were so young and . . . Whatever our reasons, we shouldn't have done what we did."

"Forgive you for what, Mama?" He decided to take a page from Nikki's playbook. "You did what you thought was best for me. Even if it wasn't." He leaned over and hugged her tightly.

Elizabeth walked into the room. "I can't believe your house, Mrs. McMann. It's simply lovely."

"That's very kind of you," his mother said as they broke their embrace.

"I can't believe it's the first time I've been here." She turned to Lucas. "Shame on you for not sharing this wonderful house with me."

"It is wonderful and so full of history. It's been in the McMann family since before the Civil War." His mother sighed. "Of course, it's not easy to keep a house that old up to par. But I do my best."

"Mama, if the house is getting to be too much for you, let Suzie take it over," Lucas said. "She'd love it. At your age, you shouldn't be worrying about this monstrosity."

"What should I be doing at my age?" There was a warning in her tone, but she said it with a smile.

"Anything you want, Mama. Anything you want." He turned to Elizabeth. "Do you think that was the right answer?"

"I do indeed. Good save."

"That's why I'm a politician."

"I just got off the phone with the Charlotte office of the FBI."

"And that's my cue to leave. This old gal is taking a nap. I've had a busy day." She hugged Lucas and then turned to Elizabeth. "It's so nice to have you here. I wish it were under better circumstances." She left the room, as regal as ever.

"What did the FBI have to say?" Lucas turned to Elizabeth. "Have they found out who the shooters are?"

"Not yet, but they're making progress, or so they claim. It didn't sound like much to me. They didn't find any fingerprints at your cabin, but they found some tire tracks. How that'll help, I don't know. But they claim it will."

"We have to give them time to work."

"I suppose, but I'd feel a lot better if they found them. Who knows if they'll try again?"

"I've got an agent protecting me. Everything will be fine. It's been a long day, Elizabeth. I need to get a little work done before I go back to the hospital to check on Nikki."

"I'll come with you. After all, I am your assistant."

"I need to be alone." Lucas walked to the guesthouse, hoping he hadn't hurt Elizabeth's feelings too much. It had been way beyond the call of duty to come, and he appreciated it. But he needed some time to himself — to think and to pray.

As soon as he was in the house, he picked up the Bible on the stand beside his chair. Nikki's words had pierced him. How had she seen into his soul and found that dark, black space where all his ugliness lived? He remembered her words. She'd told him that she'd forgiven him and God had forgiven him but that he needed to forgive himself. When he'd heard her speak those words, he hadn't reacted, but he'd known she was right. He'd been carrying guilt for so long, it had skewed his thinking. Somewhere along the way, he'd started believing he was responsible for everything. That he could control everything. But he couldn't.

That was God's job.

Lucas's Bible opened in Philippians. He scanned through several chapters and then he saw it.

"But one thing I do: Forgetting what is behind and straining toward what is ahead."

He read the verse again and again. He'd spent his life doing just the opposite. Always looking to the past. Never looking to the future. And certainly not enjoying the present. He'd been blessed with so much, and he'd never taken the time to enjoy it. All he'd ever done was follow the path his father had set for him. He moved to another verse in the Gospel of John.

"If the Son sets you free, you will be free indeed."

Tears welled up. Jesus had freed him, but he hadn't left the jail cell. Instead, he'd kept closing the door, refusing to step out into the freedom. He didn't have to live in his self-imposed prison.

God wanted him to have a future.

And it could be the future Lucas wanted. Not the one his father planned for him. A future without politics? A future where he didn't worry about the public's reaction. A future filled with love and laughter. Hard to imagine. But it was something to think about.

His cell phone rang "The Star-Spangled Banner." It was a special ring reserved for only one person. He hit the button. "Hello, Mr. President."

18

"I can walk by myself." Nikki shrugged her sister's hand off as she helped her out of the car. She was ecstatic the doctor had finally released her. She'd ended up having to stay two extra days, thanks to an infection. But he'd assured her she was just fine now.

If only people would stop hovering.

"I'm just trying to help. You don't have to bite my head off."

Immediately contrite, Nikki grabbed hold of her sister's arm. "Sorry about that. I know you're trying to help. I guess that nurse was right when she said I wasn't a good patient."

Bethany patted her arm. "That's OK. After all you've been through, I guess you have a right to be a bit cranky."

"I have no such right, and I'm grateful to be out of that place so my sissy can take care of me." She leaned against her sister's shoulder. "Thank you, my sweet Bethie."

Bethany smiled. "You haven't called me that in years."

Ray walked out to meet them. He took hold of Nikki's other arm. "There she is and looking beautiful even after being shot. What a woman."

"No need to go overboard with the pampering."

"Are you sure? I've got my famous lasagna baking, but if you don't want to be pampered, I can find someone else who will appreciate it."

"I never said I didn't want a little pampering." There was no mistaking the aroma of the lasagna when she walked in the house. Her mouth began to water. "A doctor and a cook. Bethie sure knew what she was doing when she hooked you."

"Don't kid yourself. I'm the lucky one." Ray smiled at his wife as he pointed towards the family room. "The sick bed's ready and waiting for its guest of honor. We even added extra movie channels to the cable for the month."

"I don't plan on being here for a month."

Ray smiled. "You will be here as long as it takes to get you well. No arguing about that, Nikki. And there are books on the coffee table too. Nothing for you to do but relax and get healthy."

After she got comfortable on the sofa, she grabbed the remote. It was hard to believe with so many channels, she couldn't find something to watch.

"Auntie, you're out of the hospital." Cassie bounced into the room.

"In the flesh." She turned down the volume.

"Awesome."

"Awesome indeed."

Bethany came in, a vase in each hand. "Hey, sweetheart. Set up the TV trays. We'll eat in here." She set the flowers on the coffee table. "There's two more vases out in the kitchen. I'll bring them in later."

"Wow, Aunt Nikki, you really rate. Mom never lets us eat in here. Even though it's the family room. You do know Mom's a fanatic about cleanliness."

Nikki nodded. "I do know that about her."

"That's not true. If you're sick, I let you eat in here," Bethany protested.

"Yeah, but then I can't really enjoy it. Everyone else eats in their family room. Nikki even eats in her living room, if you can believe that. You really need to loosen up, Mom."

"There's nothing wrong with keeping a house clean. Would you really want to live in a pigsty?"

"There's a big difference between a pigsty and clean enough to operate in."

Bethany rolled her eyes but smiled. "I suppose there is."

"Time for my lasagna," Ray yelled from the other room. "Need a little help."

After dinner Cassie stood up. "I have two more important questions and then I have things to do."

Nikki looked at her. "What do you want to know?"

"First, where is the great congressman? I guess he hightailed it back to DC. He must have felt safer there."

"In case you didn't watch the news, he had to go back to help get the budget passed or the government would shut down — again."

"Hmm. Likely story. Second question — do you have the hots for him?"

Nikki felt the heat rise up to her face. "Why would you ask such a ridiculous question?"

"The flowers, for one thing." Cassie pointed at the bouquets Bethany had placed all around the room. "Those are not 'get well' flowers. Those are 'I love you' flowers."

"Don't be silly. I haven't seen the man in . . . in years. He's just being nice. After all, I did get shot because of him."

Cassie turned to her mom. "What do you think, Mom? Get well or I love you?"

"I must admit they are quite extravagant."

Nikki gave her sister a little kick. "You both are wrong. I think they are 'feeling guilty about getting you shot' flowers."

Cassie and Bethany laughed.

Nikki pointed at Cassie. "Go . . . go do your homework. Or something." When she'd left, Nikki looked at Bethany. "I know she's not always the easiest, but you and Ray have done a great job."

"Thanks, Nikki." Bethany sat down beside her. "We need to have a talk about . . . about Lucas."

Nikki shook her head. "There's nothing to talk about."

"Oh yes, there is."

The doorbell rang.

"I've got it," Ray yelled as he walked to the door.

Nikki hoped it wasn't for her. Since the news had broken, she'd received a dozen calls from old classmates.

"I didn't know you were coming," Ray said.

Who was it?

"Is it a problem?" Lucas was here.

"Oh, my goodness. I'm a mess." Nikki

panicked.

"You look beautiful." Bethany rolled her eyes. "Besides, what do you care? It's only Lucas."

Ray opened the door. "Our patient has company."

"I wish I had my camera," Lucas said, eyeing the sisters, who were still hugging.

"I thought you didn't like pictures."

"I love pictures of other people, especially one as sweet as that." He placed a white bouquet of flowers on the coffee table beside all the others. "These are for you."

"The other ones haven't died yet," Nikki said. "But thanks. These are beautiful."

"Yeah, I wonder what kind of flowers those are, sis." Bethany stood up.

Nikki rolled her eyes. "Don't worry about what kind they are."

Bethany started laughing and then Nikki joined in. Soon the two were laughing uncontrollably.

Lucas looked at Ray.

"Sisters. Don't even try to understand their humor."

"I guess."

Bethany turned to him, still laughing. "It's nice to see you, Lucas. It's been a long time."

"It has. You have a lovely home."

"Thanks so much." She turned to Nikki. "I'll leave the two of you alone."

Nikki gave her sister a hard stare. "Make sure Cassie doesn't disturb us."

"Why?" Lucas stared at Nikki.

"Why what?"

"Why can't Cassie disturb us? She's obviously very important to you, and yet I haven't met her? It almost seems as if you don't want me to meet her."

Nikki's face flushed red. "Don't be ridiculous. Why wouldn't I want you to meet her?"

"That's what I was wondering. What's wrong with her? Three heads or something worse?"

"Oh, something much worse. She's a teenager." Nikki grinned.

"Well, one of these days I plan to meet her." He sat on the sofa beside her. "Thanks for calling to let me know you were released."

"You had important things to do."

"They weren't any more important than you."

"I planned to call you before I went to bed."

"No need to now." He held up his hands. "I'm here."

"So will the government shut down again

or did you save us in the nick of time?"

"Nick of time. We passed the budget a few hours ago." He smiled at her. "I missed you."

"So what's the news with the FBI? Did they catch the bad guys yet?"

Nikki seemed determined not to talk about personal issues.

The good news was she couldn't get away from him. Sooner or later, he would have his say. "Unfortunately, nothing. They're following up on the emails but this guy is good. They assure me that they'll get him. But it will take some time."

"In the meantime, you're still a target."

"It's you I'm worried about."

She lifted her arm. "I'm fine. Look, I can still pitch a softball. It hasn't hurt my range of motion. I just have to take it easy for a while."

"I still wish you'd let me hire some security for you."

"No. And that's my final word. Stop asking me."

"I didn't come to talk about security or the FBI."

"Then what?"

"I came to thank you."

"It's not necessary."

"You don't know that. You don't even

know what I'm thanking you for."

"I assume for getting shot instead of you."

"Wrong. I came to thank you for telling me to forgive myself for Victoria's death."

"Oh. Well, did it do any good?"

Their gazes met.

He nodded. "After spending some time with God, I decided you were right. I'm not the one in control. God is. Victoria and I were simply in the wrong place at the wrong time. It wasn't my fault."

She smiled at him. "How does it feel?"

"Pretty good. In fact, very good." He picked up her hand.

"God is so good."

"One of the things I figured out when I was in all those boring meetings is that I'm ready for a new chapter in my life."

She pulled her hand away. "That's good, Lucas. From what Elizabeth said, that's about to happen."

"I'm not talking about politics. I'm talking about us." He wouldn't let her change the topic. "I already told you once that you're the only woman I ever fell in love with. I always thought about you. Wondered if you were happy. Wondered if you missed me. Even after Victoria and I learned to love each other, I wondered about you."

Her eyes filled with tears. "Lucas, we're

212

both grown-ups now. We had a lot of fun, but we were kids. But that's all it was — puppy love." Picking up the glass of water, she sipped through the straw.

"Puppy love. That's what you call what we had."

"OK, maybe we even loved each other in spite of how young we were. But it was a long time ago. It has nothing to do with the present."

"It wasn't that long ago."

"Long enough, Lucas. We live in two different worlds. I mean, really, the President called to ask for your help." She wiped at the tears falling down her cheeks. "You belong in that world. I don't."

If she didn't care about him, why was she crying?

"But I want us to live in the same world."

She met his gaze and shook her head. "It can't happen. We're too different."

Lucas heard her words and knew she meant them, but he could see the love in her eyes. He didn't understand what the problem was. She'd forgiven him, and they'd moved past those old hurts. He wanted a life with her. Maybe it was too quick for her. He shouldn't have surprised her like that. One small step at a time instead of one giant leap. He could be patient. After all, he worked for the government. "Can we at least be friends?"

She grabbed the box of tissues. "We are friends, Lucas."

That was a start. "Friends visit each other, so that means I'll see you soon."

"No more flowers."

He shrugged. "I'm not making any promises. I'll keep you posted on what's going on with the FBI investigation."

"Hopefully, they'll find out who is behind this so you can get back to your real life."

He smiled at Nikki, knowing she was his real life. If only he could convince her that they were meant to be together. If only he could break through that wall she'd built. But those were mighty big ifs!

Nikki was sitting on the bed when someone knocked on the door. "Come in."

"Hey, little sis. Just checking to see if you need anything before I go to bed."

"Not a thing."

"Is it OK if we talk for a minute?"

Now what? The last thing she wanted was another heart-to-heart. Of course, she couldn't blame her sister. Bethany must be worried to death about Lucas coming to the house. Might as well get it over with. "Don't worry, Bethany. I know Lucas can't keep coming over to the house. I'll find a way to stop it."

"What is it you think you know?"

"I have no plans to get involved with Lucas. I wouldn't do that to . . . to this family. To you." Nikki lowered her voice.

Bethany closed the door behind her. "Do you have feelings for him?"

That was a good question. One she'd been avoiding answering even to herself. "It doesn't matter if I do."

Bethany sat down. "It does matter."

"All that matters is that Cas— that this family stays intact."

"If this is the man who will make you happy, then we'll figure it out. Our family, and that includes you, is strong enough to withstand the truth."

Nikki didn't believe that for a minute. The truth would devastate Cassie. She shook her head. "How can you think that I would ever want to be with him after . . . after what happened?"

"What really happened, Nikki? Think about it. What did Lucas do that was so awful? You broke up with him because Mom and Dad made you. He didn't break up with you."

Nikki adjusted her position so she could look at Bethany. "I know you're right, but he could have defied them. Instead he left me to face . . . to face . . . well, you know what I faced."

"But he didn't know about it. You can't keep blaming him."

"He would have known if he'd come to see me even once. And I am not blaming him. I've forgiven him." She smiled at Bethany. "It feels so good to not be angry at him anymore."

"It wasn't his fault, Nikki. In fact, we may have been the ones who did the unforgivable." Her sister's voice was quiet, reflective.

Nikki stared at the ceiling. Those were tough words to hear, but her sister was right. "Even more reason why we can't ever have a relationship. It's too complicated. It's all in the past. Let's leave it there."

Bethany wiped away tears. "I want you to be happy. And if Lucas can make you happy, we'll figure it out. We'll make it work out."

Nikki leaned over and hugged her. "You are the best sister ever. I love you and I appreciate that you want me to be happy, but Lucas McMann will not ever be a part of my life."

"If that's what you want, fine, but don't be a martyr. You have as much right to be happy as anyone else."

Could Lucas make her happy? She shook her head. "Can you see me as a senator's wife at a cocktail party in a fancy dress? I think not. The fanciest thing in my wardrobe is a glittery T-shirt."

Bethany whispered in her ear. "I think you would make a wonderful wife to Lucas or to any man you choose." She walked to the door. "Sweet dreams."

Nikki lay in the dark. There would be no sweet dreams that night. How could she not have realized that before? Could she really be that selfish and unfeeling? Apparently so. For so many years, she'd made herself believe she'd been the one betrayed by Lucas. Now she had to face the truth — she'd betrayed Lucas, not the other way around.

He had a right to be angry at her. And he didn't even know it.

She turned onto her good side and curled up in a ball, allowing the tears to come as she prayed for forgiveness. The tears washed away the years of anger and the bitterness. The deceit she'd participated in when she'd been so hurt she didn't know where to turn. Even as her heart healed, she knew Lucas still couldn't be a part of her life.

He would never forgive her if he found out the truth about Cassie being his child.

And rightfully so.

She could admit to herself that sometime in the past few days, she'd fallen in love with him all over again. But they could never have a future together.

Decisions had been made the night Cassie had been born. Decisions that had changed their lives forever. And it was too late to un-change them.

Nikki lay in the dark, staring at the ceiling. It may not have been the right thing to do, but they'd done it. And it had worked out.

Bethany and Ray loved Cassie. They had created a wonderful life for her baby — the baby she couldn't take care of.

Perhaps, if she'd gone to Lucas. Told him the truth, everything would be different. But she hadn't. Now she would have to live with her choices — and part of that choice included not telling Lucas. It would be just as wrong to try to rectify her mistake for her own selfish desires.

In the dark, Nikki whispered, "God, forgive me."

19

Nikki opened her eyes. She'd tossed and turned most of the night. But sometime in the wee hours, God had given her the grace to forgive herself. Her heart overflowed with peace and joy along with an expectant excitement that God was working in her life. It was amazing, and she wanted more of that kind of love.

God had a great plan for her life.

Her Christian mentor had told her this, but she hadn't felt the truth of that promise until now. And even though she still loved Lucas, she was at peace that he couldn't be a part of her life. Now all she had to do was to figure out what it was God wanted her to do.

Was Lucas right about a flower farm? She closed her eyes and imagined herself surrounded by flowers, digging in the dirt, creating beauty from a seed. It was a pretty picture, but she wasn't sure. It might take a little time to figure out what she should be doing. She followed the scent of cinnamon to the kitchen. "Morning, Bethany."

"Just in time. The muffins will be ready as soon as I put a little icing on them."

"How about a lot?"

"Did I say a little? I meant a lot. I don't have to ask you how you slept — I can see. You look exhausted. They shouldn't have let you come home yet. Maybe you weren't ready."

"Oh, I was more than ready to get out of the hospital. I wouldn't have slept any better there. It may not have been the best night's sleep, but not to worry, I feel wonderful." She walked over to the coffeepot and poured a large mugful.

Cassie rushed into the kitchen, holding her laptop. "I found it. I found it."

"Found what?"

"It wasn't easy. It took me most of the night but I found it. Then I fell asleep. I just woke up or I would have been down sooner. Can you believe it? I found it!" She grabbed a muffin and took a large bite. "I love Mom's nutty-cinnamon muffins. She really is spoiling you."

"They are tasty. Now, tell me what you found."

Cassie dove into the refrigerator and came

out with a jug of milk. She took a glass from the dishwasher and plopped in a chair. "After you told us why Mr. McMann hired you, I started searching on the internet. I put in all kinds of search words. *Games. Famous people. Pictures. Photographs.* Any word I could think of. Nothing."

"You didn't have to do that."

"I told you computers are my thing. If Mr. McMann thought he was the victim of some sort of cyberstalking, I wanted to find it." She poured milk and bit off another chunk of the muffin at the same time. "And besides, somebody shot you. They need to be arrested and the key thrown away."

"Don't talk with your mouth full. So, what did you find?"

"At first nothing, but then I thought about it. What would make people take pictures of someone for someone else?" Another bite of the muffin. "The answer — money."

"Of course. That makes sense."

"I started searching for sites that offered money for photos and eventually found this." She turned her laptop towards Nikki. "This is the Connecting Bridge." She pointed. "Ever hear of it?"

"Sure, it's one of the sites that keeps me in business. People connecting with long-lost loves, then thinking the grass will be greener on the other side. All it usually does is lead to heartache and divorce." She wondered what was going on with Stanley and his wife.

"I don't know about that, but I finally found this site." She pointed at the screen.

Do you live in Washington, DC, or North Carolina?
Want to make some money?

"*I* don't see anything about Lucas." She hated saying his name within hearing distance of Cassie.

"Gotta read the small copy. Here, I'll read it for you. Maybe your old-lady eyes are too bad."

"My old-lady eyes are just fine." She pulled the laptop closer.

Want to make some EASY CASH?
I'll pay for each photo you send me of senators, congressmen, and other politicians in the DC area, especially for North Carolina politicians. Email me to find out this month's target.

Nikki looked at Cassie. "Still doesn't say Lucas's name."

"True, but I emailed the person. The

email site is no longer active, but I was able to access old emails."

"You accessed someone else's email account. That doesn't sound legal." Nikki's eyes narrowed as she stared at Cassie. "How did you do that, may I ask?"

Cassie gulped the last of her milk and then smiled. "Don't ask."

"I don't want you doing illegal things — ever." Bethany walked over to the table.

"Your mom is right. That's not the way to find out who is responsible for shooting me."

"Like I said, don't ask." Cassie picked up another muffin. "Anyway, when I got access to the email, there was only one target. It was the same target month after month."

"Lucas?"

"The one and only."

Nikki grabbed another muffin. Cassie was right; they were tasty. "Now all I have to do is find out who set up the Bridge site and the email."

"I'm sure the FBI will be able to do that." Bethany wiped away some crumbs.

"Already did!" Cassie said triumphantly.

Bethany shook her head. "You and I will be having a long talk about following the law, little missy."

"Don't you want to know who it is?"

"It would serve you right if I refused to listen, but I did get shot. So I guess I have a right to know. Who is it?" Nikki took a sip of coffee and then set down the cup.

"Well, that wasn't easy either."

Bethany glared at Cassie. "Stop bragging."

"She did a good job hiding it, but eventually, they had to pay with a credit card. And she did."

"She? It's a woman?" Nikki hadn't even considered that possibility. She'd simply assumed it was a man.

"And not just any woman. Someone who knows the congressman." Cassie beamed at the two of them.

"Lucas, who are all these strange people on my property?"

With all that was going on, he wasn't taking any chances with his mother's safety. "I hired a few security guards."

"I would have thought the FBI agent would be more than enough to keep watch on you."

He didn't want to admit they weren't there to keep an eye on him, but on her. "You're probably right. I overreacted, but I've already paid for them for the next few days, so they might as well stay." Lucas walked out to the screened-in porch, or as

Mama called it — the veranda. In that sweet Southern drawl of hers, just saying the word drew a picture of time gone past. "You outdid yourself, Mama."

The furniture had been pushed to the perimeter of the room. Each of the four tables was surrounded by five chairs. The white linen tablecloths contrasted with the rose-colored antique china. Atop each of the plates sat a teacup and saucer. A small flower arrangement decorated the center of the table.

"It does look nice, doesn't it?"

"And you do this every month?"

"I like to show that gracious Southern living isn't dead quite yet."

"That's good, Mama. Nothing wrong with traditions."

"It's so sad these days. Most young women are too busy climbing up the corporate ladder to enjoy the finer things in life."

"It's a different world than you grew up in, Mama."

"Doesn't mean it's better."

He grinned. "Doesn't mean it's not. Women like the freedom they have these days."

"Humph. I had plenty of freedom. Along with that freedom comes responsibility. And as far as I'm concerned, too much responsibility. I liked it just fine and dandy staying home and raising the young'uns while your daddy went out and slew the dragons."

"And that was fine and dandy unless you were a woman who wanted to go out and slay her own dragons."

"Humph." She held up her hand. "As the young people today say, whatever!"

He laughed. "I see you aren't completely behind the times, Mama."

Elizabeth walked in. "Your mother is not behind the times at all, Lucas. How dare you insinuate such a thing?"

"Thank you, Elizabeth." His mother turned to Lucas with a haughty stare. "I'm glad someone appreciates me."

"Oh my, Mrs. McMann. The tables are beautiful, simply beautiful. Wherever did you get those gorgeous flowers?"

"From my gardens."

"Just lovely."

"If you want, after the other ladies leave, I'll take you on a tour. The gardener does most of the work these days, but I still get my hands dirty every now and then. Nothing like a little warm dirt on my hands to remind me where I came from."

"That would be lovely."

As far as Lucas knew, the only dirt Elizabeth ever put her hands in was political.

But flower gardening? He didn't think so. Nikki was the one who loved growing flowers.

The doorbell rang.

"They're heeeere." Lucas smiled. "I better get going while the going's good."

"You aren't staying?" Elizabeth looked disappointed.

"No way. This is ladies' day." Besides, he wanted to visit Nikki for a while. Baby steps.

"The last time I looked, women had the right to vote," Mama said.

Elizabeth smiled. "Your mother's absolutely right. Every one of these women is a voter. Along with their husbands, children, grandchildren, and great-grandchildren."

"That may be so, but I'm not in the mood to politic today." He waved as he walked through the door. "Have a wonderful time, ladies. Enjoy your tea."

Nikki drove towards the McMann mansion.

The police cruiser in front of her held two officers. After Cassie's discovery, Nikki had visited the police station and shown them the evidence. A call to the FBI agent assigned to Lucas's case had developed the strategy for arrest. The police weren't too pleased that she insisted upon being there, but conceded in light of her involvement and injuries, with strict warnings for her to stay out of the way unless they specifically asked her for help. An emergency warrant was issued within a half-hour.

The woman had hired trained assassins to kill Lucas, and after some careful research, the police had determined right where she happened to be.

Attending a tea party at Isabella Mc-Mann's home.

They waited outside the gates until given the all clear that almost all the women had left the party. Although women in the cars coming out gave the cruiser a cursory glance, no one looked at Nikki's car parked right behind it.

Nikki followed the cruiser into the long circular drive. Her gaze landed on the white-pillared monster, and suddenly she was sixteen again. Her heart pitter-pattered as she remembered the dinner where she met his parents. What a nightmare that had been. Lucas had insisted she come to Thanksgiving dinner at his house. She'd never attended a formal dinner before. When she sat down and saw all those forks, spoons, and knives, she hadn't known what to do.

His mother had been kind to her and

shown her what piece to use at the right time.

Even as young as she was, she could tell they weren't pleased with their son's choice. And she understood why — she wasn't good enough for Lucas — or for them. Her address was on the wrong side of town.

Shaking away the bad memories, Nikki took a deep breath. No longer a child, she was finally beginning to know who she was. A child of God. And that made her worthy. Her income or her address didn't matter to God.

Nikki walked towards the mansion. She wouldn't let the house or the people intimidate her — this time. She wasn't sixteen anymore.

A man in a suit stood in front of the door, talking with the officers. Must be one of the FBI agents guarding Lucas. One cop gestured to her as she got out of her car.

"I'm the one who took the bullet for the congressman." Nikki walked up to the men.

An officer rang the doorbell.

A minute or so later, the door opened and a dignified white-haired man in a suit stood there. His smile disappeared at all the badges being held up for him to see. "Can I help you?"

"We need to see Mrs. McMann and her son."

"This is not a good time. Perhaps you could contact them later."

"This is a warrant for the arrest of one of the guests, and we will accompany you inside."

"I will get Mrs. McMann for you." The butler opened a door, revealing a room with only a few women standing around Mrs. McMann. From their body language, they were saying their goodbyes.

The aroma of flowers battled with the scent of tea. The tables were filled with nearly demolished trays of small sandwiches, cookies, and petit fours along with several different teapots.

The chatter came to an abrupt stop as the policemen, the agents, and Nikki followed the butler in.

The white-haired man made a small motion. "Madam, these officers wish to speak with you and Mr. Lucas. I told them to wait at the door, but they refused."

"Thank you, Butler." Isabella McMann moved towards the officers and Nikki with a friendly smile and an outreached hand. "Gentlemen and Ms. Kent, it's very nice to see you again. Is there a problem?"

Nikki stared at the woman who wanted

Lucas dead. The woman responsible for her getting shot. The woman looked at her for a moment and then quickly looked away.

"We're here with a warrant to arrest one of your guests." The officer was gracious. "We waited until nearly everyone had left, thinking we'd cause less commotion that way."

"What has . . . she done?" Mrs. McMann asked, looking at the few remaining women behind her.

"She's responsible for attempting to kill Lucas and shot me instead," Nikki said.

The knot of women gawked at them with frank curiosity.

At Nikki's bold statement, one woman sank into a nearby chair, hands fluttering.

"Ma'am, is your son here? We know he may be able to shed some light on this issue too."

"He is, but he refused to come to my tea party." Her blue eyes twinkled for a moment before turning sober again. "I can't imagine why."

"You can fill Lucas in later." Nikki kept her gaze focused on one specific woman. "Let's get started, shall we?" Nikki walked around the room and reached Elizabeth.

The officers moved to the target too.

Lucas came in with the other FBI agent.

"Nikki, what's going on? Butler said there might be a problem."

"Butler? Can't you at least call him by his name?"

"That is his name. Butler Davis."

"Oh." How did she manage to always make herself look foolish? "Well, good. Anyway, I'm glad you're here. I've found out a few interesting facts. I know who's responsible for me getting shot." She looked at Elizabeth.

Elizabeth jumped up. "How dare you accuse me of such a thing?"

20

There was no way Elizabeth could be responsible for the stalking or the shooting. He trusted her with his life. Nikki had it wrong.

Nikki put a hand on Elizabeth's shoulder. "Relax. I didn't accuse you of anything. It's not you — it's her." She pointed at the woman sitting on the other side of Elizabeth.

"You must be mistaken. That's Victoria's sister. She would never —" Mrs. McMann actually sputtered.

"Kathryn Rites, you have the right to remain silent . . ." The officer recited the rest of the official Miranda statement.

"I don't know what you think you know, but maybe we should go somewhere to discuss this." Kathryn's mouth trembled, her face pale. "Not here."

Mama's face was just as pale, her mouth twisted in shock. But it was the look in her

233

eyes that gave Lucas a pause. Lucas recognized that expression on her face. He'd only seen it a few times in his life, and none of them had been pleasant.

"Kathryn, if you tried to hurt one little hair on my son's head, you deserve jail time. And you had the nerve to come to my house. To my tea party."

Lucas put a hand on his mother's shoulder. "Mama, let's just hear what Kathryn has to say."

"I don't have anything to say."

The officers circled Kathryn.

Nikki set the laptop on the table. After pushing several buttons, a picture popped up. She turned to Lucas. "Here's the website where she offered to pay for every photo people could take of you. I'm sure as the FBI digs a little deeper, they'll connect her with the credit-card fraud as well as the assassination attempt."

"Kathryn, how could you do that to Lucas?" His mother swayed.

He helped her to a chair. "It's OK, Mama. It's over now. Why would you do this to me, Kathryn? We're family." Lucas was bewildered.

Kathryn stood up and lifted her chin in defiance. "My sister's dead. Why should you have a life when she doesn't?"

"I tried to save her."

"You didn't try hard enough. She wasted her life married to a man who didn't love her."

"I loved Victoria."

Her laugh was brittle. "You ruined her life."

"How can you say that?"

"She wanted children. But all you cared about was your career. You made her a trophy wife instead of the mother she wanted to be."

"We loved each other."

"She loved you. I'll give you that. But you? You don't love anyone but yourself and your career. The great Lucas McMann."

"Kathryn, it wasn't like —"

"Whatever. So what if I paid some people to take pictures of you? It's not illegal. The paparazzi do it all the time."

The FBI agent moved between Lucas and Kathryn. "True, but conspiracy to murder is against the law."

"Murder. I didn't try to murder anyone. I don't know what you're talking about."

"Sure you did." Nikki was angry. "He didn't die in the robbery, so you went after him again to make sure he died. Your assassin missed and shot me instead."

"Assassin? I don't know —"

"How could you come here and pretend to be a part of my family?" His mother stood, her blue eyes blazing.

"Isabella, I didn't do any such thing. She's lying. All I did was pay for some stupid pictures. I wanted someone to knock that smug smile off his face, not kill him."

"Ma'am, you'll need to come with us." The policeman was still polite.

Kathryn backed away. "Why? I didn't do anything illegal. I paid for some photos. That's all."

"Well, somehow the harassment went from photos to someone shooting." Nikki glared.

"Don't you understand? He ruined my sister's life."

"We had a good life together." Lucas stepped forward, puzzlement in his expression.

"A good life." Kathryn sounded disgusted. "Don't you understand? All she wanted was to be a mother. You stole that from her."

"You're wrong, Kathryn. That was her decision, not mine. I wanted children. Always did. She's the one who refused."

Uncertainty flickered in Kathryn's eyes. "It's still your fault. Why would she bring a child into a loveless marriage?"

"Our marriage wasn't loveless. It might

236

not have been the breathless love of romance novels, but it was love. Strong and true. And when she died, I mourned her."

"Mourned her?" A tear trickled down Kathryn's cheek. "I hardly think so. You went back to work without skipping a beat."

His mother stepped to his side. "Each of us mourns in our own way, Kathryn. Because he went to work didn't mean he wasn't grieving."

Both policemen moved to Kathryn. "Please put your hands behind your back."

"No." She jerked away from them. "I haven't done anything to be arrested for. What's the charge?"

"Conspiracy to murder." The officer waited a beat and then reached for her arm. "Please comply and put your —"

"Get away from me." She jerked away. "You can't arrest me. I have rights."

Each of them grabbed one of Kathryn's arms.

She struggled against them to no avail. Within seconds, she was handcuffed. "Lucas, I didn't try to kill you. I don't know what they're talking about. You have to believe me."

He looked into Kathryn's eyes and he did believe her. Yet Nikki had the proof. Something was wrong here. "Let's find out all the facts before we become her judge, jury, and executioner. I'm going to Charlotte."

Elizabeth stepped closer and put a hand on his arm. "I think your mother needs you."

"Lucas, you go do what you need to do. I'm fine." His mother motioned at the room. "Besides, I have to clean up my tea party. Thank you, officers, for waiting until the end of it to come. I assume that's what you did."

"Yes, we did." The officer smiled at her. "We didn't want you to deal with a ruckus here, Mrs. McMann."

"Nikki, you've got this wrong." Lucas sat across from Nikki at a conference table in the FBI office. They were waiting for the agent.

"I've shown you the proof. I understand it's difficult to believe your sister-in-law is responsible for all of this, but that doesn't change the facts."

"I agree she's responsible for the photo stalking or whatever you want to call it, but there's no way she hired someone to kill me. This is a woman who goes to tea parties and PTA meetings. She wouldn't even know how to hire a killer."

It did seem odd. She had to agree with

Lucas about that. As improbable as it seemed, Kathryn Rites was responsible for her getting shot. "I'm sorry, Lucas. I don't know what you want me to say. You can believe it or not, but she set up this website. They have the credit-card transaction that proves it."

He stood up, clearly frustrated. "I just can't believe this. Kathryn has never been anything but kind to me."

Agent Sarah Goode walked in. She held out her hand to Nikki with a smile. "I don't mind telling you we don't like civilians getting involved in our cases. But I made an exception in this case. Thank you so much for your help."

"You're welcome. Glad to be of service."

"Is Kathryn being charged?" Lucas stood up.

"For harassment and stalking right now. She's admitted to that, but she's adamant she had nothing to do with the shooting. Don't worry, we'll keep digging. Sooner or later, we'll find the connection."

"Maybe she's telling the truth."

"It's possible. And if that's the case, we'll find that out as well. Your brother-in-law wants to talk to you."

Lucas looked at Nikki. "This will only take

a few moments. Then we can talk some more."

"I'm exhausted. I'm going home."

Worry and concern filled his eyes. "Of course you are. You're still recuperating. You should be home resting. Maybe I should drive you."

Nikki had to admit it was nice to have someone to take care of her. Not that she would let that happen, but it was still nice. "I'm fine, Lucas. I can drive myself home."

"If you're sure." He hugged Nikki.

For a moment, she leaned against him, savoring the feeling.

"Then I'll talk with you tomorrow." He left.

Sarah Goode shook her head. "What a tough situation."

"He's having a little trouble accepting the facts."

"He'll come around. Thanks again for your help."

"You're very welcome." Nikki nodded as she turned to leave.

Agent Goode called to her. "Oh, by the way, if you're ever looking for a job with the FBI, let me know. I'll smooth the way for you."

Nikki turned back. "Really? Did you see my Army records?"

The agent smiled. "I did happen to see those, and my offer still stands."

"Thanks. I may just take you up on it." She walked out of the office.

Lucas and his brother-in-law were in deep conversation.

She stepped into the elevator and exited on the level where her car was parked. As Nikki walked through the underground parking lot, she shivered. Even with her training, no woman liked to be in a dark place alone. It was something hardwired into their DNA as a safety net, she supposed.

Footsteps pounded on the cement behind her.

She turned back and pulled her keys out so she could get into her car quickly. As she neared her vehicle, unseen hands grabbed her. Instead of falling, her face smashed into the side of the car.

"I won't hurt you. Just listen." His voice was a hoarse whisper.

"Let me go." She struggled against his hold.

He rammed her into the car hood. "Go back to Florida. The congressman isn't the man you think he is. He can't be trusted. Being around him could be hazardous to your health."

Something jabbed into her arm.

He let go of her.

She turned around, but everything went woozy. Through blurred vision, she saw the back of a man running. *The needle . . . had to get him . . . needed to find out . . .* She fell to her knees . . . Nikki opened her eyes. Did she faint? The jab. That man had drugged her. How long had she been passed out? She remembered his words.

The congressman isn't the man you think he is. He can't be trusted.

Not just words, but a warning.

Lucas had shown her just the opposite. He'd protected her. He'd carried her when she couldn't walk. He'd saved her life. Not only saved her life, but had been kind to her in the face of her own anger.

The man was wrong about that.

But maybe the man knew something else about Lucas that he was trying to keep hidden. Maybe all of this had nothing to do with Kathryn Rites. Instead, it was about Lucas and politics.

Nikki stood up, her mind confused and jumbled from the drugs. She needed to go back into the FBI office. She stumbled towards the elevator. After taking a few steps, she stopped, totally exhausted. Her arm throbbed and her head hurt. She wasn't going to make it. She'd rest in her car for a few minutes and then try again. She barely made it back. Climbing into the vehicle, she slumped against the seat, determined to try again when she could stand.

Lucas sat at his desk now scattered with papers.

He wasn't in the mood for work. He spent some time answering emails on a variety of topics.

Tap, tap. Someone knocked on the door.

"Come in."

Elizabeth entered.

His security guard stepped into the room, holding the door.

In spite of Kathryn's arrest, they were still taking precautions.

"Evening, Elizabeth."

"I had a few things to discuss with you if you've got the time now that you're back."

"I've got nothing but time. Come in." He looked over at the security agent. "Do you want to come in? You'll be a lot more comfortable."

"No thanks, Mr. McMann. Just making sure you know I'm here."

Lucas didn't like the knowing smile the man gave him. "Well, if you or your partner need to, just come on in. No need to knock."

That should make his relationship with Elizabeth clear enough.

"I thought we might as well get a little work done if you're up to it." She held up her tablet notebook.

"Sounds like a plan."

They worked through several upcoming issues and what his response would be. After a heated discussion about using this mess in his upcoming election, they moved to his computer to take care of some of the more crucial emails. As they worked their way through the emails, Lucas saw one with *MUST SEE* in the subject line. He skipped over it.

"That one says it's a must-see. You better check it. It could be important."

It was for his eyes only. "I'll check it later."

"Are you sure? They used capital letters."

"I'm sure." He moved to the next email. After a few hours of working, Lucas stretched. "I've had enough for one day."

"Me too. Sorry to be such a slave driver."

"It seems like there aren't enough hours in the day to get all the work done. Let alone time to relax or even enjoy a ball game once in a while."

"That's what happens as you move up the ladder, Lucas. But you're right. It is important to relax. If it's too much, I can always hire another assistant for you. Especially when you become a senator."

It wasn't so long ago that seemed like the most important thing in his life. But he wasn't sure about that any longer. "Let's hold off on that for now, but I'll keep it in mind." After she left, Lucas clicked open the email.

Three photos. All of Lucas. First, Lucas leaving the hospital. Lucas in his mother's car at the florist. And the last picture was of him walking into Nikki's sister's house. Below the third picture in large capital letters was written a message.

GO BACK TO WASHINGTON BEFORE SOMEONE ELSE GETS SHOT! THIS TIME, IT MIGHT BE YOU!

He picked up the phone and dialed Sarah Goode's personal number.

A moment later, she answered.

"I'm sorry to bother you, Agent Goode. This is Lucas McMann."

"Not a problem."

"I received another email."

After describing it, Sarah said, "Well, that's certainly to the point, isn't it? What's the time on that email?"

"Three hours ago."

"There's no way Kathryn Rites could have written that. She was in custody."

Even though the email added to the mystery, he was glad to know his sister-in-law wasn't responsible for it. "You know what that means, don't you?"

"That we have the wrong person in custody? At least for the shooting."

"I can't figure out what they want from me. I thought they might have wanted me to resign my position. But if that were the case, they wouldn't tell me to go back to DC."

"I agree. It might be more personal than we think. Is there anyone in your personal life who might want you out of here and back in DC?"

And away from Nikki. "Not really." As he stared at the screen, it went blank. "And now it's gone."

"What do you mean?"

Lucas explained what happened.

"We have a really great tech guy. I'll call him to come out there and perhaps he can figure out how they're doing that."

"Nobody else has been able to."

"Well, he will, or at least, I hope so. Unfortunately, he's out of town. But the minute he gets back Monday morning, I'll have him come out."

"There's something else I've been thinking about."

"What's that?"

"That night at the cabin. I was there for quite some time before Nikki came. I was walking out on the deck and was a perfect target."

"And . . ."

"And why didn't they shoot me then?"

"Maybe they weren't there yet."

He nodded. "That's possible or maybe . . ."

Agent Goode finished his thought. "Or maybe you weren't the target. Maybe the real target was Nikki Kent."

"And if that's true, then Nikki's still in danger."

21

Nikki sat on the edge of her bed at Bethany's house. She was tired and exhausted and wanted to go home to Florida, where she could climb into bed and collapse. There was something she needed to do but she couldn't quite grasp it. The man, the needle jab, something had gone haywire. She started to do something but got tired. And when she'd woken up again, she'd driven home, barely able to stay awake.

Would this never end? This went much deeper than a McMann family issue.

The attack last night meant it wasn't over.

Maybe Lucas was right and the problem wasn't Kathryn Rites.

An epiphany went off inside her mind. She should have called the FBI last night. But Agent Goode had given Nikki her cellphone number too. She'd call her soon.

Bethany and Cassie were at church and Ray was at the hospital.

She'd enjoy one last day with her family and then go back to Florida tomorrow.

The FBI had taken charge of the situation. There was nothing more for her to do.

And the sooner she was away from Lucas, the better. He muddled up her thinking. Their time together had been too intense. It brought back too many memories that needed to be forgotten.

She walked downstairs. Fresh coffee and the last of the nutty-cinnamon muffins sat on the counter. A note was emblazoned with her name.

Look out the front door. B

She walked to the front door and opened it.

A strange man stood at the door.

"Who are you?"

A moment later, Lucas walked up the steps with a bouquet of flowers. "Good morning." He handed her the flowers. "For you."

"Why are you here and who is that man?"

"I'll explain everything if you let me come in."

She opened the door wider. "You don't have to give me flowers every day."

"It seems only right, considering what I keep putting you through."

"You aren't responsible for the actions of

other people."

"I agree, but I like giving you flowers anyway. After all, one of these days you might just become the flower lady."

"I just got up." She pointed at her pajamas.

"So I see. Nice look."

"I need some coffee." She walked back to the kitchen and poured a cup for both of them. She stared down at the muffin. Only one. "I'll share."

"Not necessary. I already had my breakfast. Coffee's fine."

After sitting down and taking a few sips, she looked at him. "OK, why are you here and who's the man?"

"He's FBI."

"FBI? I told you I didn't need any babysitters." Her tone was too harsh. She smiled to offset her tone. "It's not that I don't appreciate it, but it's not necessary." Well, maybe it was, considering what happened last night.

"I wasn't taking chances with your safety. Agent Goode and I had a talk last night and we became a bit worried about you. She decided you needed some security. Not me. If you're upset, talk to her."

"You've been here all night?"

"No, just since about two this morning.

When I called Agent Goode."

"Did you get any sleep?"

He took a sip of coffee. "How sweet of you to be worried about me."

How could he be so happy without any sleep? She needed her solid eight hours before even thinking about being cheerful. "I suppose this is as good a time as any to tell you I was attacked last night in the FBI parking garage."

He set down the coffee cup and stared at her. "You were what?"

"I was walking to my car and someone pushed me down."

"And I'm just now hearing about it. Are you hurt?"

"As you can see, I'm fine." No need to tell him they'd drugged her.

"Why didn't you tell anyone?"

"I was so tired. I just wanted to come back here. I planned to call Sarah today." She stared at him. Should she tell him what the man had said? Did it even matter?

"I knew it. I knew you were in danger. I don't care what you say. You're keeping the security."

"I can do that for today, but I'm going back to Florida tomorrow."

"Tomorrow? Why so soon?"

"I've done all I can here. The FBI doesn't

251

need my help to get to the bottom of this."

"That's probably a good idea. You'll probably be safer in Florida, but before you go, we need to have a serious talk. I know a lot of time has passed, and I know I hurt —"

"There was nothing to forgive."

"I wouldn't say that."

"I would. If you remember, I'm the one who broke up with you."

"My father gave me a choice, college or you. The next day, you called and told me you didn't want to see me anymore, so I went to college." Lucas sighed. "Several years later, he told me the truth, but by then, it was too late. You were married."

"See, I'm right. You really did nothing to be forgiven for. You were a victim." More than he would ever know.

His gaze met hers. "We were both victims, Nikki."

Her heart thumped. She wanted to go to him, have him put his arms around her and tell her everything would be all right. Instead, she smiled at him. "Good. That's all settled."

"And that brings us to the present. All the secrets, all the hurt is behind us."

Nikki didn't want to talk about secrets. "Now we can both move on with our lives."

"I agree. And there's no reason we can't

do that together."

Oh, there was a big reason. "Lucas, that can't happen. It's a sweet, romantic idea, but it's not practical. And you know it."

"Love isn't supposed to be practical."

He was making this so hard.

"Maybe not, but someone has to be. I'd like to pretend that it could work. That we could have a fun and exciting whirlwind romance. But in the end, it still wouldn't work."

"Why not?"

"To make it very simple, before the end of the year, you'll probably be a senator in DC. Where you belong and I don't."

"I just don't understand why you aren't willing to give it a chance. To give us a chance."

Her heart was breaking but she had to do this. For Cassie. "You will always have a part of my heart, but we are not meant to be together."

"You're wrong, Nikki. Please give us a chance." He bent his lips to her. "I love you."

She didn't move away. She wanted him to kiss her forever. When they separated, she shook her head. "I loved the you I knew when I was sixteen. And you loved the me that I was then. We can treasure what we had, but it's time for us to move on with our lives. I can't be a senator's wife and you can't be a private investigator's husband."

"That does sound ridiculous when you put it like that." He looked at her and brushed her hair away from her cheek. "We can find a way to make it work."

She shook her head. "No, we can't." She picked up her coffee cup and walked to the sink.

"Are you sure?" He moved closer.

She forced herself to step back. "I'm sure."

"If you ever change your mind . . ." He touched her cheek once more.

The silence between them grew. He put a hand on her shoulder.

She closed her eyes, savoring the feeling of his hand on her, knowing it would be the last time.

With a light caress, he touched her hair. "If you change your mind, you know where to find me." In Washington, DC — where he belonged.

As much as she'd like to change her mind, she wouldn't. Cassie came first. When she heard the door open and close, she let the tears fall.

By the time Bethany came back, Nikki was showered and dressed.

"I see the guard is still here." Bethany set her Bible on the coffee table.

"Just for the day. He'll leave when I leave."

"That's certainly nice of Lucas."

"He's FBI, not a security guard Lucas hired. Besides, I got tired of arguing."

Bethany laughed. "You, tired of arguing? I guess you really have changed." She sat down in the recliner.

"Very funny. Where's Cassie?"

"I dropped her off at the library."

"I didn't know kids still went there."

"Her English teacher gave them some sort of assignment that could only be done at the library. She wants them to learn how to use it. And not just the internet."

"I thought you'd like to know what happened yesterday."

Bethany leaned forward. "I was being polite, waiting until you brought it up. So did Kathryn Rites get arrested?"

"She did, but we aren't sure if she was the one responsible for me getting shot."

Her eyes widened. "What do you mean?"

"Well, at first we thought the case was closed. Until I was attacked and drugged, then —"

"You were attacked and drugged?" Bethany jumped up from the chair.

"Don't get yourself in a panic. As you can

255

see, I'm fine."

"No wonder Lucas insisted on having security with you. I don't think you should go back to Florida."

"But that's what the mugger wanted me to do."

"Since when do you let someone bully you?"

"I don't, but that's what I planned to do anyway. So, I'm not being bullied into not doing what I'd already planned."

"I think that makes sense." Bethany sat back down. "The truth is, the farther you're away from Lucas McMann, the safer you'll probably be."

She didn't know about safer — but it certainly was easier. It was just too hard being around Lucas and knowing they could never be together. She nodded. "It's my last day. What do you say; want to go eat at the diner?"

"Sounds good to me."

When they returned, Bethany looked at her watch. "I can't believe Cassie's not home yet. She should have been home over an hour ago. Unless she's in one of her moods again."

"Any reason she would be?"

"She doesn't need one. Anything can set her off at any time." Bethany picked up the phone and hit a number. As she waited, she rolled her eyes. "She's not answering her phone. I hate when she does that."

"Maybe she turned it off since she was at the library. You know, you're supposed to be quiet there."

A few minutes later, the doorbell buzzed.

"I'll get it, Bethany." Nikki hoped it wasn't Lucas again. But she was pretty sure it wouldn't be. He seemed to have gotten the message. There was nothing more either of them could say. The past was over and they each had a future but it wouldn't be together. She opened the door. "Rachel."

Cassie's best friend stood there, her face streaked with tears. She was out of breath. "I . . . I . . . they grabbed her. Put her in a van."

"What are you talking about?"

"Cassie. They kidnapped her."

"Did she say *kidnapped*?" Bethany's voice rose and cracked.

"Tell me what happened." Nikki led the sobbing girl to the sofa.

"Cassie left the library first. I was trying to catch up to her. She was a few blocks away when a van stopped. Someone got out of it and grabbed her. At first, she was fighting, but then she sort of collapsed. I was running as fast as I could to get to her. To help her. They put her in the van and drove off. I screamed for help but no one came." Rachel dissolved into tears.

"Did you call the police?"

"Didn't have my phone with me. I forgot it. I just came here."

Bethany had turned pale and looked as if she couldn't breathe.

"Bethany, call 911. Now."

Lucas sat on the sofa, pretending to read the newspaper while his mother watched TV. In reality, he was thinking about Nikki. Something didn't fit. He could tell she had feelings for him. He could see the love in her eyes. Yet she refused to acknowledge that. She kept talking about them living in different worlds, but so what? That only made them as a couple more interesting, not impossible. He smiled at the thought of introducing Nikki to his stodgy friends as a private investigator. Could his ego be telling him that Nikki felt the same way as he did, but in reality, she was over him? He sighed.

Mama gave him one of her sidelong glances. She probably could tell something was wrong, but she wasn't hounding him. She'd wait until he was ready.

He wasn't ready. Nikki had asked him to respect her wishes, and he would do that.

For now. But he wasn't giving up. He was sure God had a plan for them — together. He turned another page of the paper and tried to focus on the words.

The TV broke in with an Amber Alert.

When he heard the word *Maiden,* he looked up from the paper.

His mother's hand flew to her mouth. "Oh, my goodness. Who is it?"

Then the picture flashed on the screen.

Lucas stared, not believing his eyes. His baby sister, who died of meningitis when she was four years old, stared at him . . . older, but with the same flaming red hair and bright blue eyes. This was what Mary would have looked like if she'd lived. Had she . . . he looked at his mother, not understanding. Then he heard her name — Cassie Martin. "That's Nikki's niece. But she looks just like Mary. How can that be?" He looked at his mother. "Did you see her? Doesn't she look just like Mary?" The expression on his mother's face scared him.

Tears filled her eyes, but she still didn't speak.

"Mama, do you see her?"

"This is . . . this is horrible. Her family must be worried to death."

"How can Nikki's niece look that much like Mary? I don't understand."

His mother took a deep breath and then met his gaze. "Because she's not really Nikki's niece."

He sat down on the sofa, not able to breathe. Not able to think. Finally, he found his voice. "What are you saying, Mama?"

"She's Nikki's daughter."

Lucas stared at his mother. Nikki had a daughter. A daughter who was sixteen. How could that be? The pieces of the puzzle clicked into place. It couldn't be true. "And. . . . and I'm her father."

His mother nodded but didn't look at him.

"I have a daughter. And you've known about it."

"Only for a few years."

"And you never told me. How could you not tell me, Mama? I had a right to know. She's my daughter."

"She is Ray and Bethany's daughter. They are her parents. No matter who had a part in creating her, she is their daughter. We don't have the right to shatter that child's life because of our own selfishness."

"How can you say that? She has a right to know I'm her father."

"She has a father and you aren't him." His mother met his gaze.

"How can you say that?"

"Because I've had a lot of time to think

260

about it. To pray about it."

"You never thought Nikki was good enough and I guess her daughter . . . my daughter, isn't good enough either."

"Stop right there, Lucas McMann." She stood up and faced her son. "Don't you think I wanted to hug my grandchild the first time I saw her? Just like you, I knew immediately she was a McMann with that flaming red hair and the picture of Mary. Don't you think I haven't lain awake at night praying for guidance, praying that telling you was the right thing? And every time I did, the answer came back the same. Cassie doesn't belong to me or to you."

Anger coursed through him. He would have never thought his mother would have hidden such a thing from him. Betrayed him like this. His father, yes. But not his mama. "You know how much I've wanted a child."

"And now you have one. So act like a parent. Put your child's needs ahead of your own." Her blue eyes blazed with righteous anger. She wasn't backing down.

He was tempted to throw the fact in her face that she'd let his father's needs take precedence over her son's. But that wasn't true. He'd wanted to please his father. That had been his choice.

A choice that had left Nikki alone and

pregnant.

Oh, dear God. He sent his thoughts heavenward.

No wonder she had been so angry and bitter. She'd had to give up her child because he hadn't been man enough to stand up against his father.

No wonder she'd kept Cassie away from him.

It all made so much more sense now.

What had he done? With shaking knees, he sat back down on the sofa. "Doesn't Cassie have a right to know who her real parents are?"

"She knows who her parents are. And it's not you and Nikki Kent. For whatever reason, Nikki made a decision. In spite of what we did, she could have come to you and told you she was pregnant. Or she could have come to us and asked for more money. But she didn't. She put that child's needs first. And as much as you'd like to, you haven't the right to tell that child anything different."

"But she's been kidnapped. Am I supposed to sit here and do nothing? Pretend I don't know who she is?"

"Of course not. Go put every resource you have into finding her. And when she's found, you'll step back and let her family

262

celebrate her homecoming. Her family, not yours."

"But I'm her father."

"Then act like it."

His first act as a father was to call Elizabeth. He left a message for her. "Elizabeth, I have an emergency. It's not me. I'm fine. But I need you to do something for me."

"Just when you need her, she's not answering. Lousy timing." His mother paced.

"Chances are she's in or near a national forest. No cell-phone reception. It happens all the time to me when I drive here."

"The TV reporters didn't give many details. Can you call Nikki to find out what happened?" his mother asked.

"Better yet, I'll drive to her sister's house."

She put a hand on his arm. "I know it's not my business and I have no right to ask, but I am. Please don't upset them any more by telling them you know the truth. This isn't the time."

Could he do that? Could he really pretend he didn't know? He wasn't sure if he could keep the masquerade up forever, but his mother was right. They didn't need more stress at the moment. He could keep quiet now.

Cassie's parentage wasn't what was important. Finding Cassie was all that mattered.

"I'm not asking you to lie. Just keep quiet. Once you've had time to think about it, you'll know the right thing is to not disrupt Cassie's life. Think how betrayed she'll feel. She'll feel as if everyone important has lied her whole life. Think how horrible that would be."

"I won't say anything right now. But I'm not promising I won't later. When she's safe. But for now, I'll keep quiet."

His mother kissed his cheek. "I know you'll do the right thing after you've had some time to think about it. Pray about it, Lucas. God will tell you what He's been telling me. Do not disrupt that precious child's life." She left the room.

Lucas walked over to the mantel and slipped the picture of Mary into his pocket. He walked out the door and got into his car.

As he drove to Ray and Bethany's house, he tried to still his mind, but it was going a hundred miles per hour. To discover that he had a daughter, and that there was an Amber Alert out for her. Mind-boggling.

When he arrived at the house, there were two police cruisers and several other vehicles. He pulled in. Trotting up to the house, he prayed for calmness and courage. But most of all, he prayed for wisdom.

22

Her life had morphed into a living nightmare. Nikki stared at the circus in Bethany's dining room.

Two uniformed officers, one county deputy, as well as the chief of police. Rachel. Rachel's mother. Ray and Bethany, of course. All of them were talking at the same time. Bethany, Rachel, and Rachel's mother took turns crying.

Nikki wasn't crying, but it was taking all her strength not to. How could this have happened? She had a sick feeling that it had something to do with her "warning" last night.

Rachel answered every question the officers threw at her with as much detail as she could remember. She looked over at Bethany. "I'm sorry, Miss Bethany. I should have been with her. This is all my fault. I shouldn't have stopped to talk to Mark. If only —"

"Don't do that, Rachel. It's not your fault," Ray said.

Tears slid down Rachel's cheeks. "It is my fault. It is . . ."

"Why would someone want to kidnap Cassie?" Bethany laid her head on the dining-room table and sobbed.

Ray rubbed her back. Pain was etched in his face. "I don't understand it. We aren't rich."

Nikki didn't understand it either.

The chief of police sat in an empty chair across from Rachel. "Rachel, I need you to look at me."

Rachel looked up.

"I need the truth. Understand?"

She nodded.

"Maybe Cassie told you to tell her mom and dad this story. When the truth is she ran away again." He gave the teenaged girl a hard stare. "Are you sure this really happened?"

"No. No. You've got to believe me. I'm not making this up. I saw them put her in the van. She didn't run away. They took her. You've got to find her."

Bethany jumped up. "You need to stop accusing her and my daughter of things that aren't true and go find her. That's what your job is. Not to threaten Rachel into admitting something that's not true."

Ray put a calming hand on her arm. "Bethany, they have to ask these questions."

Bethany shook off his hand. "No, they don't. They need to understand how serious this is. Not make false accusations."

"Ma'am. No one is accusing them of anything. We're simply asking the questions that need to be asked."

"What are you doing to find her?" Bethany turned to the chief and wailed for answers.

Nikki moved to her sister's side but said nothing.

"We're doing all we can. We've got the Amber Alert out. Dark-colored vans all over the state are being stopped and checked."

"Why isn't the FBI here?" Ray asked.

"There's a protocol we have to follow. First us, then the county, then the state. And then finally the FBI, if warranted."

"I don't care about your protocol." Ray glared at the detective. "That seems like a waste of time. We need the FBI."

"I can assure you the FBI will be involved if we need them. Right now, everything's being done that can be done."

"I don't see anyone doing anything except standing around here," Bethany said between sobs.

"Not true. We've got all your phones ready to be traced and recorded if there's a ransom call. Someone is checking traffic cams and security cams, looking for the van. If we can get a license-plate number, we'll find that van."

More sobs from Bethany. "I don't want the van, I want my daughter."

The doorbell rang.

Nikki opened the door.

Lucas stood there. "I heard about Cassie on the news."

Their gazes met.

Time stood still. She couldn't breathe.

The truth was in his eyes. The pain and the knowledge shone through. Lucas knew Cassie was their daughter.

In the blink of an eye, her world tilted. "I . . . I . . ." She couldn't find any words. "I . . ."

"I'm here to help, Nikki." He put his arms around her. "I will always be here to help you. No matter what."

She rested her head against his chest. The years of separation melted away. It was just the two of them. Together. Nikki whispered, "Forgive me."

"No, forgive me. I left you all alone."

"I already have. How did you know?" She stepped out of his embrace.

Lucas reached in his pocket and handed her a picture. Nikki stared at it. The girl looked like a much younger version of Cassie. Bright red hair, but with more freckles and that infectious grin. Nikki's gaze moved to Lucas. "I don't understand."

"That's my sister, Mary. She died when she was four from meningitis."

"I . . . I . . . I . . ." Her thoughts were jumbled. "Your mother met Cassie the other day. She knows?"

"She's known for a while. After seeing her sing at some church event. It only takes a look at Cassie to know she's got McMann blood in her. But she didn't think it would be good for Cassie to know. According to Mama, it could rip her life apart."

"I agree with her. That's why I've been . . . been keeping my distance." Nikki wiped away the tears. "I'm sorry. I didn't mean to . . ." That wasn't true. She had meant to keep the truth hidden from him and from Cassie — forever. Her gaze met Lucas's. "I can't do this right now."

"Of course not. We can talk about this later. Right now, I'm here to help."

"It's a mess. Everyone's arguing about everything. I don't think they know what to do. Ray wants the FBI called, but they keep saying it's not warranted."

269

"Has there been a ransom demand?"

"Not yet."

"Money won't be a problem. I can cover whatever amount they ask for."

"That's . . . that's . . ." She had no words to express her gratitude.

"What happened?"

Nikki told what she knew.

"It's a good thing her friend saw it happen. Otherwise, no one would have any idea she'd been abducted."

Nikki walked over and sat on the couch. "I'm missing something. This makes no sense. Why would anyone want to kidnap Cassie? Bethany and Ray have a little money but they aren't rich. Not rich enough to pay a ransom."

"Maybe it's not about money."

"Then what could it be about? I'm just not getting it. There has to be a logical explanation, but I'm not seeing it. Is there any way to get the FBI involved?"

"Will do." He walked out of the room. "Let me go talk with the chief."

A moment later, her phone vibrated. She pulled it out of her pocket. It was a number she didn't recognize. "Hello."

"If you want to see her alive, you'll do exactly what I say." The voice was distorted.

Panic filled her, but she pushed it away.

She'd dealt with two kidnappings before and she knew one thing. Emotions could get the victim killed. Forcing her voice to be calm, she asked, "What do you want?"

"Get in your car right now and leave. Take your phone with you. Just you. If anyone else comes, she's dead."

"Let me talk to her."

"Leave now."

Lucas walked into the dining room. He saw the shocked looks of most of the people in the room and ignored them as he walked over to Bethany and Ray. "Bethany, Ray, I'm so sorry about all this."

Bethany clung to her husband's hand, wiping tears away.

Ray nodded. "Thanks, Lucas."

"Nikki said the FBI haven't been brought in yet, but that's about to change." He paused. It wasn't his place to take charge. He looked at Bethany and Ray. "If that's what you want."

"That would be great, Lucas." Bethany pointed at the police chief. "But he doesn't think it's necessary."

"Is that all right with you, Chief?" Lucas didn't really care what the man thought, but if he could help him save face, he would.

Much to his credit, the man smiled. "That

would be great. All we want is to bring Cassie home. But as you know, the FBI have their protocols."

Lucas nodded even as he was dialing Sarah Goode.

He briefed her on the situation and she agreed to help. "Thank you so much, Agent Goode. I knew I could count on you."

"One question before you go, Lucas."

"Of course."

"Do you think this girl's kidnapping has something to do with what's being going on with you?"

The question shocked him. But was it possible? After all, he'd only had to look at Cassie to know she was a McMann. Someone could have decided to use her to get to him. "Why would it?"

"No reason. I just wanted to check. I'm walking to my car and I'll be in Maiden as soon as I can get there."

"Thank you, Agent Goode." Lucas pressed the end button.

All eyes were staring at him. Bethany and Ray's eyes showed gratitude. Rachel's were hopeful. The chief of police's didn't show either.

"They'll be here soon." He walked back to the living room.

No Nikki. She probably needed to freshen up.

He sat down on the sofa. Sarah Goode's question haunted him. Could Cassie's abduction have something to do with him?

Nikki shot. Nikki attacked and drugged. Nikki's niece abducted. No, not niece. Nikki's daughter. His daughter. All along, he'd thought this was about him. But maybe it was about Nikki. Nikki seemed to be the target. During her mugging, they'd warned her to stay away from him. It wasn't just about him or just about Nikki. It was about both of them. Someone didn't want them together.

He pulled his phone out and hit the number for his mother. He updated her on the situation and then ended the call. Elizabeth still hadn't returned his call. He wanted her to find a kidnap expert whom he could hire. He tried her number again. Still no answer.

Lucas paced the living room. He walked over to the large picture window that was the focal point. He imagined Cassie growing up here. Happy and secure with a mother and father who loved her. In that moment, he knew Nikki had made the right decision for Cassie all those years ago.

A child deserved a happy home and parents who not only loved her, but could provide love and security. Even if he and Nikki had stayed together, they wouldn't have been able to take care of Cassie the way she deserved. They were practically children themselves back then. As much as he'd loved Nikki, he hadn't been able to stand up to his father.

Yet Nikki had found it in herself to do what was best for Cassie. The pain she must have endured through the years as she watched their daughter grow up. No wonder she was so angry when he'd walked into her office. Still staring out the window, he focused on the scene in front of him. Something was different.

Nikki's car was gone. She'd left? Without telling him or anyone? She wouldn't do that unless . . .

He didn't like where his thoughts were going. He pulled out his phone and scrolled through the numbers. He double-tapped Nikki's number. It rang and rang until it went to voice mail.

There could be only one reason she'd left and not told anyone. The kidnappers had contacted her. Why would they have contacted Nikki instead of Bethany and Ray? It made no sense. Except it all came back to Nikki once again. Nikki was the target. She was in danger.

Lucas walked into the dining room to tell them of this new development. He opened his mouth but then closed it. He had no idea what the kidnappers had told Nikki or if they'd even called her. He didn't want to get anyone excited if that wasn't the case.

If something happened to Nikki or Cassie, he would never forgive himself.

Nikki was a smart woman. Over the years she'd been in all sorts of situations. She could handle herself.

Lucas trusted her. "I'll be back in a bit. Call me if there are any developments." He turned and walked out before anyone could ask any questions.

His FBI guard stood at the door.

Lucas explained the situation. "Agent Goode is on her way. In the meantime, I'd like you to come in to offer assistance in any way you can."

"Of course, sir."

Lucas waited until the man disappeared into the dining room and then he walked to his car. He had to keep Nikki safe.

Nikki drove aimlessly down the road, not sure where the kidnappers wanted her to be. Maybe she should have told the police they'd called. Or at least told Lucas, but the man on the phone hadn't given her a choice. She wouldn't risk Cassie's life — no matter what.

Her phone rang again.

She glanced over.

Lucas, just like the other seven times.

As much as she wanted to talk with him, include him in what was happening, she couldn't. Besides, by now he'd probably told everyone she'd left. It wouldn't take long for them to figure out the kidnappers had called.

The police had a certain way to handle situations. But this wasn't the time to play by their rules.

Cassie's life was at stake.

Nikki would do what she had to do to keep her baby safe. Even if it meant skirting the law. Or making Lucas angry. None of that mattered. Only Cassie mattered.

The phone stopped ringing.

She breathed a sigh of relief.

The phone rang again.

She glanced at the screen. The kidnappers. Grabbing up the phone, she pressed answer. "Hello."

"Are you alone?" The same distorted voice as before.

"Yes."

"Where are you?'

"I'm on Route 150 North."

"And you're sure no one is with you?"

"Just me." And her gun. "Let me talk to Cassie."

"Don't worry about her. She's fine. Go to Lincolnton."

"Let me talk to Cassie."

"Your daughter's fine."

"Let me —"

The phone beeped as the caller disconnected.

Nikki pounded her fist on the steering wheel. "Lord, keep her safe. I don't care what happens to me, but please keep her safe."

The phone rang.

Lucas again.

Lincolnton was in the opposite direction she was going. After making sure there were no cars in either direction, Nikki made a U-turn. A few moments later, she heard the sirens.

A cruiser pulled in behind her.

"No. No. No." She didn't have time for this. Nikki pasted a smile on her face as she rolled down her window. She pulled out her license, registration, and concealed-carry weapons permit. "Good afternoon, Officer."

"License and registration."

"Yes, sir. I need to advise you I have a gun

in the car and a permit to carry it. Here it is." She handed him her documents. Thank heavens, she had a permit for Florida and that it was reciprocally honored in this state. Telling him about the gun was the protocol for anyone with a conceal-and-carry weapons permit.

"Where's the gun?"

"In the console between the seats." Her phone started ringing. "I have to get that."

"No, you don't."

"You don't understand. I really do have to get that. I'm a private investigator and I'm —"

"I don't care what you are or what you're doing. Please follow my directions."

The ringing stopped.

Nikki closed her eyes, praying Cassie would be OK.

A car pulled in front of her. Just what she needed. Another circus and she was the main attraction.

The occupant held his license out the driver's side window. "Officer." The driver raised his voice. "I'm Congressman Lucas McMann. May I step out of the car? I am unarmed."

"Ma'am, step out of the car and put your hands on the hood." The officer stepped back.

Nikki got out and walked to the front of her car, putting her hands on the hood.

"Sir, you may exit the vehicle." Even as he talked with Lucas, the officer watched her like a hawk.

Lucas got out with his hands held clear of his body. "Thank you, Officer." He leaned closer. "Officer Jenkins. I'm Congressman Lucas McMann."

"Yes, sir. I vote for you every election. My parents love you too."

"That's great to hear." Lucas shook the patrolman's hand. "Is she being arrested?"

"Not at all. Just a precaution. She told me there was a gun in the car and gave me her permit. When you drove up, I made her get out for my protection. Can't be too careful these days. I had to make sure you were who you said you were."

"Makes sense. I can assure you everything's legal. She's working for me. Did you hear about the shooting I was involved in?"

"Of course."

"Ms. Kent is following up on a lead. Time is of the essence."

"Maybe I could help."

"You can help by letting her get on her way."

"Of course."

"Am I free to go?" Nikki asked.

"Of course. You have a burned-out tail-light. It's legal in this state to only have one, but I simply stopped you to advise you to get it fixed, since it may not be legal in Florida. I saw your license plate." He turned to Lucas. "It's nice to meet you, Congressman."

"And it's nice to meet you. Do you have a card? I'll call your commanding officer and tell him what a good job you're doing."

"Oh, that's not necessary." He grinned. "But it would be awesome if you did. Thanks so much, sir." He fished a card out of his pocket and handed it to Lucas, then walked back to his cruiser.

Lucas took hold of her arm. "I'm assuming the kidnappers called you."

"I've got to get going. I'm supposed —"

"I'm going with you."

"You can't. They told me I had to come alone. We can't take a chance on them seeing you. I won't do anything to endanger Cassie."

"And you think I will?"

"That's not what I meant. I know that you wouldn't."

The police cruiser pulled out, leaving them alone.

Lucas waved as he drove past. "Then let's get going."

"That's not happening."

"I'm not let —"

"I can handle myself."

"I know you can. I've seen you in action, but I'm still not leaving you."

"Lucas, you have to let me do this on my own."

"You're not alone. I'm here with you."

"Well, you can't be seen. If you want to ride in the trunk, I guess you can."

"Not a problem."

She stared at him. "Don't be ridiculous. I only said that to make you go away. I didn't really mean it."

"Except I'm not going away." He walked to the back of her car. "Pop the trunk."

"I will not pop it. You can't ride back there. It's not safe."

"It is safe. This is a fairly new car. It probably has an inside trunk release. Most do these days."

Her phone rang. She held up a finger to shush him as she grabbed it off her seat. "Hello."

"Why didn't you answer?"

"Because I was being detained by a state patrolman who didn't like the way I was driving."

"You should have been more careful."

"I was following your directions." She gritted her teeth and reminded herself that she didn't want to make the man angry. "But you're right. Careful will be my middle name now."

"I changed my mind. Go to Hickory, take 70 to Statesville, then 77 South to Charlotte." At least she had a location now.

Her phone beeped off. She really needed this guy to stay on the phone for more than fifteen seconds. She had to get him to let her talk to Cassie. She turned to Lucas. "Gotta go."

"What did they say?"

"Not much. They told me to get on Highway 21 North and then hung up. I don't have time for chitchatting. I have to get moving."

"True. Pop the trunk or I will."

She glared at him. "Fine. But you better get the keys out of your car or someone will have a fun joyride. Your mother won't be happy."

"Good point." He turned back to his car.

Nikki slid into her driver's seat, quietly shutting her door. She turned on the ignition and at the same time put the car in drive. "Sorry, Lucas. I have to do what they say."

Another vehicle was in her lane. She had to beat it if she didn't want Lucas following her. Pressing on the gas, her car surged forward. As she turned onto the highway, her car fishtailed. With both hands, she attempted to get it under control. A glance in the rearview mirror showed the too-close car behind her fishtail as well. And then a horn blasting. And another. She righted the car. The speedometer moved upwards. Seventy . . . seventy-five . . . eighty . . .

23

The nearly disastrous scene unfolded as if in a movie.

He felt foolish because he'd allowed Nikki to trick him so easily and terrified she would kill herself trying to get to Cassie. She surged past cars as if they were sitting still. Then she was gone. The kidnappers had told her to come alone, and that was exactly what she planned to do.

He should have known she wouldn't give up that quickly. He slammed a fist on his hood. Not that he blamed her. He'd have done the same thing if they'd contacted him. But he wasn't letting her face those kidnappers alone. It was time she had someone she could count on.

She'd been alone and afraid at Cassie's birth because he hadn't been man enough. He hadn't been there when she needed him the most, but he'd be there this time. He'd find her one way or another.

Getting in his car, he waited for the traffic to clear. At least he knew the general direction she was going. She must not have been thinking clearly when she told him where they wanted her to go. Or maybe she had been thinking clearly. Just maybe, she'd told him wrong. It didn't matter. It was his only chance, so he'd take it and hope for the best. He pulled onto the road, trying to figure out his next move — or actually Nikki's next.

Guide me, God . . .

After passing more cars than he could count, he realized Nikki was gone. The question now was how to find her.

His phone rang.

Maybe she'd had a change of heart and decided to include him. As he picked up the phone, he knew that wasn't the case. "Hello, Elizabeth."

"Lucas, what's going on? I got your message, but it wasn't very clear. What's wrong?"

"Nikki's niece was kidnapped. I want you to hire a K & R expert and get them down to Maiden as soon as possible."

"A kidnap and ransom expert? Are you sure about that? After all, you told me she'd gone all the way to Florida without her parents' permission. What . . . when did this happen?"

"I'm sure. I don't have time to explain. Contact Agent Sarah Goode from the Charlotte FBI office. She can give you any information you need. Just get those K & R experts down here. Cost is not a factor."

"Of course, I'll do anything I can to help."

"One other thing. I need you to track a phone number and tell me where it is."

"Why?"

"No time to explain. Can you do it?"

There was a long pause before Elizabeth answered, "Of course I can do it. Well, actually, I can't, but I know someone who can."

"Good enough. And please don't tell anyone else about it. This is between you and me. Call me back as soon as you know where the phone is."

"Lucas, where are you? Please, don't do anything dangerous. Let the police handle this."

"Don't worry about me. Just hurry and get the location of that phone. I need it right away." He rattled off the number and pulled over. He prayed, begged God to keep them both safe.

The phone rang. "Hello."

"Lucas, this is Agent Sarah Goode."

"Yes, Agent Goode."

"Where are you? What's going on?"

"Nothing's going on. Why would you ask that?"

"Because you and Nikki Kent disappeared."

"We're driving around." That technically was true. Even though they weren't driving around together. "She couldn't sit in that house another second. We're looking for dark-colored vans." All true.

"With all due respect, that's my job, not yours."

"I know that, and if we find one, we'll contact you right away. It's just that Nikki had to do something." That was certainly true.

"I can believe that. I get the feeling she's not one to sit on the sidelines."

"That's for sure."

By now, Lucas was far behind. Nikki couldn't let him catch up. Keeping her gaze on the speedometer and her foot on the gas, she moved through the traffic. Fast enough to stay ahead of traffic, slow enough not to get stopped by another state patrol. Moving to the slow lane, she waited for the next exit to come up. She couldn't take the chance of Lucas catching up. He wouldn't be as gullible next time.

Her phone rang. "Hello."

"Where are you now?"

"I'm getting very tired of this cat-and-mouse game. Tell me where you want me to go and I'll go. And let me talk to Cassie. If I don't know she's . . . a . . . ." Her voice faltered, not even wanting to say the words aloud, but she took a breath. "If I don't know she's alive, I'm done."

There was a long pause. "Fine. Hold on."

Another long pause. "Aunt Nikki, I'm —"

"Satisfied. Now follow my instructions. Take 21 South to Charlotte. Get off the first Charlotte exit and go to the corner restaurant. When you get there, go to the trashcan, leave your phone, and you'll find an envelope under the trashcan with your final instructions. That's how you'll find your daughter."

21 South. That was the road she'd told Lucas. Totally ridiculous. By telling Lucas the opposite direction, she'd inadvertently told him the right way. Well, that couldn't be helped now. She could only hope he was far enough ahead of her that they wouldn't run into each other.

Someone could be following her, tracking her every move. There were any number of ways they could do that these days. Depending on what sort of resources they had. And obviously, these people had resources. She drove back on the highway, watching for Lucas and anyone else who might be following her. "My daughter."

The kidnapper had called Cassie her daughter.

Nobody knew that. Well, almost nobody. Lucas and his mother now knew the truth, but they would never do anything like this. Had they told someone else about her? Not likely. Had someone else seen Cassie and realized she was Lucas's daughter?

That had to be what happened. And that meant this wasn't about Cassie or a ransom. Cassie's kidnapping had something to do with Lucas and the assassination attempt on his life. If that was the case, and Nikki was pretty sure it was, then Lucas was still in danger.

But that didn't make sense.

If this was about Lucas, why would they have called her and not Lucas?

He would have done exactly what she was doing. Followed their instructions to get to Cassie, and then they could have killed him and Cassie. Why hadn't they called Lucas?

Even as she drove faster than she should, she forced her mind to slow down. Think like an investigator. She sifted through the events of the past week.

According to Lucas, the picture they'd

sent of her office showed they'd known Lucas had come to her for help. The night at the cabin, Lucas had been an easy target, but she'd been the one shot. Then she'd been mugged and warned to go back to Florida to stay away from Lucas.

They knew Kathryn Rites was responsible for the stalking, but she'd maintained her innocence of the assassination attempt. Agent Goode and Lucas both thought she was telling the truth, especially after Nikki had been mugged.

Someone else was obviously involved. Someone who didn't want Nikki anywhere near Lucas.

Nikki pulled into the restaurant parking lot. She hated giving up her cell phone. It was her lifeline, but it couldn't be helped. She was at the kidnapper's mercy. She usually kept a burner phone in her car when she was working, but she hadn't put one in when she'd headed to Maiden with Cassie. She'd assumed she wouldn't need one. Boy, had she been wrong about that. Too late to worry about it now. She picked it up and opened the car door.

Stepping out, she scanned the area for trashcans. Three of them outside. One at each of the doors and one in front of the building. Going to the first one, she lifted it up. No envelope. Same at the second. Of course the envelope was at the last one. After scooping it out, she held up her cell phone for a moment and then tossed it into the trashcan. She waited until she was back in her car before ripping open the envelope.

It was empty. They'd lied to her. They had no intentions of taking her to Cassie. It had all been a ruse to get her out of the house.

Tears trickled down her cheeks. What was she supposed to do now?

They'd never intended for Nikki to find Cassie. Maybe that was the point. Maybe it was about money. In that case, perhaps Bethany and Ray had been contacted.

And Lucas was willing to give them whatever amount they needed. Lucas should be there with Bethany and Ray. But she was sure Lucas was out there looking for her. He was as stubborn as she was.

It was time to call Bethany and Ray to find out what was happening. And admit her own failure. She stepped out of her car and went to retrieve her phone. She tried not to think of all the germs as she stuck her hand in the trashcan. She may not be a germophobe like her sister, but . . .

A vehicle approached.

"Get in, now."

She turned to see an open door on a black

van. Without a moment's hesitation, she climbed in. She felt a sharp jab in her arm and then her body relaxed.

Nikki took an envelope out of the trash and then threw her phone in the garbage can. She walked back to her car with the envelope. A moment later, she hopped back out. She fished around in the trashcan again. The kidnappers had obviously told her to get rid of her phone.

Someone was probably watching.

A van pulled up, blocking his view. *Move.* He hated losing sight of her, even for a minute.

The van drove away.

Nikki was gone. Had she gone inside? She'd have had to cross right in front of him to do that. But that didn't mean she wasn't in there.

The van. The black van.

Of course. Cassie had been dragged into a dark-colored van. Nikki must have gotten in the van. She would do anything to keep Cassie safe, even letting herself be kidnapped. That van would lead him to Nikki and to Cassie.

He prayed it wouldn't be too late. He pulled through the parking lot, the same direction the van had gone. He turned right.

No taillights. Where had it gone?

His phone rang.

Elizabeth. He ignored the ringing but then realized that was a mistake. If Elizabeth tracked his phone, she could send the FBI to him. "Elizabeth."

"We finally got a track on that phone. It's at a restaurant in Charlotte. I'll give you the address."

"I don't need the address. I'm in the parking lot. What I need you to do is track my phone and then have the FBI find me. I'm on the trail of Cassie's kidnappers." At least, he prayed that was the case.

"The kidnappers? Lucas, you shouldn't put yourself in danger. Where are you? Stay there and I'll have the FBI come to you. Don't get involved in this."

His daughter was involved. The woman he loved was involved. That meant he was involved. "No time. Just have them find me."

"But —"

"Just have the FBI follow me. Gotta go." He ended the call and put the car in gear, determined to find Nikki and their daughter.

He drove down one street then the other, searching. As he drove, he realized the craziness of what he was doing. He wasn't a trained investigator or a police officer. He didn't have a clue how to find them. And even if he found them, he had no weapon. How was he supposed to protect them without a gun?

Did Nikki have her gun with her? If they took her to Cassie, she'd have some protection.

Maybe he should go back to Nikki's car and see if the gun was in there. But that would take time and he had to find them right now.

Before something happened.

24

Nikki was curled in the back of the van, blindfolded, groggy, and unable to move. *Don't panic.* She forced her mind to focus. *Help me, God. Clear my mind.* When she'd climbed in the van, someone had poked her with a needle. They'd drugged her again. She wouldn't be much help to Cassie trussed up like a Thanksgiving turkey. But this wasn't the right time to put up a fight.

First, she had to find Cassie. Then she could fight.

She prayed. She suspected it hadn't been that long since they'd drugged her. Perhaps just long enough to confuse her — keep her off balance. She was grateful they hadn't used duct tape to bind her hands. She rattled the handcuffs around her wrist.

The van slowed down, then came to a complete stop. A hand shook her. "Wake up, Sleeping Beauty. Time to die."

She kicked at the man, but only managed

to move her leg through the air.

He laughed. "Sorry, you missed me."

"I can pay you more money than whoever is paying you now."

He laughed again. "Sure you can. I almost believe that." The van door squeaked open and then he grabbed her by the arms and pulled her out. Someone grabbed her other arm.

Her arm throbbed. "I will. I promise I'll pay you anything you want. Just let me go and walk away. Before it's too late."

"Tough talk from someone who's about to die."

Nikki squeezed back the tears and stumbled along as they dragged her up steps.

A knock and then the door opened. Unseen hands pushed her hard.

She tumbled to the floor.

"Here she is. Delivered just as you requested. Now, where's our money?"

"Stay there and don't move," a voice whispered. "Or you'll die right now. Gentlemen, you've done your job well and I thank you. Here's your payment."

A moment later, Nikki heard two pings — gunshots from a gun with a silencer. Then moans. Apparently, that was the men's payment. This guy wasn't taking any chances. No witnesses. He didn't want anyone to be able to identify him. Not good. He didn't mind killing people, not even ones who'd helped him.

Please, God, let me get Cassie out of here alive.

Two more pings. Apparently for good measure.

The bag was pulled from her head.

Nikki squinted up at the kidnapper, but his face was hidden with a ski mask.

Slight of build, no wonder he'd needed help to pull this off. He didn't look as if he had the strength to take on Cassie or her.

Nikki blinked in the hopes of getting her eyes to focus. The drugs were still affecting her. She looked past the kidnapper, searching for Cassie. Her daugh— niece was crumpled up in the corner.

Please, God, don't let her be dead.

"Don't worry, she's not dead yet. I had to make sure you were here before that happened. After all, she was the bait to lure you here." The voice wasn't whispering any longer. It was a woman. No one she recognized. "But now that you've joined the party, I can take care of both of you. And then get on with my own life. I'm so tired of all this drama."

That was one thing the two of them agreed on.

"Why are you doing this? What did Cassie ever do to you?"

"Nothing. It's really all your fault. You should never have reinserted yourself into Lucas's life."

So this was about him.

"He came to me for help, not the other way around."

"Oh well. Guess you should have just said no." She aimed the gun at Nikki. "So, you want to go first or should I let you watch Lucas's daughter die? I think that's a good idea. You have been quite the aggravation to me. You deserve to suffer."

Every moment counted. Nikki had to keep her talking.

Lucas was somewhere hunting for her — for them. She had to prolong this. Give him time to find them. "How did you know she was Lucas's daughter?"

"One look at her was all it took. She's the spitting image of his sister. That's when I knew I had to get rid of both of you. Otherwise, you'd be dragging him back into your life all the time. I wasn't going to put up with it."

Who was this woman?

"At least take off your mask and look me in the eye. So I know who I'm dealing with."

"Stop trying to stall. This will all be over

in a minute." She walked towards Cassie.

Nikki slipped one hand out of the cuff and then the other, letting them quietly drop to the floor. That trick had been the talk of the police force when she'd worked there. Her slender wrists made it easy to get out of the cuffs. In one fluid movement, she jumped up, charged towards the woman, and then jumped on the kidnapper's back.

The two of them tumbled to the floor.

Nikki hit the woman in the stomach with all the strength she could muster.

The woman tried to fight back, but she fought like a girl with no strength. A moment later, the woman pressed the gun against Nikki's stomach. "Stop or I'll shoot you right now."

Who would help Cassie if she was dead? Nikki relaxed.

"Good choice. Now let go of me."

She loosened her grasp and the woman rolled away.

The ski mask had fallen off during their struggle.

Nikki stared.

The puzzle shifted. The pieces dropped into place. It made so much sense.

Lucas had been driving the back streets of Charlotte for no less than thirty minutes.

No sign of the black van or the FBI. He didn't want to admit he'd lost the only lead to Nikki and Cassie. He'd expected the FBI to show up. Elizabeth should have called them by now. Why hadn't they shown up?

He didn't have any solid information to give them. No location. Not even a license plate for it. He'd search for ten minutes and then he'd call Sarah Goode himself. Tell them what was going on, let them handle it. She wouldn't be happy, but she'd figure out what to do next. The FBI had resources he didn't have. Like traffic cams and man-power. They could do a street-by-street search for the van. It had to be somewhere around here. And that might be the only thing that would save Cassie and Nikki.

Changing his mind, he decided to call them now. He turned the corner and pulled over. As he reached for his phone, he saw the black van. He hesitated. He should call the FBI first. But that would take too much time. Nikki and Cassie needed him now. Besides, Elizabeth had already called. They would be here any minute.

He jumped out of his car, running towards the van. He opened the doors and peered inside. Empty. No Nikki. No Cassie. His gaze landed on a set of keys. Nikki's keys? He picked them up and stared at them. He was sure they belonged to Nikki.

Where had they taken her?

The van was parked directly in front of an old house. Probably abandoned since the windows were boarded up.

He ran up the steps, but approached with caution. He didn't want to alert anyone who might be inside. He put an ear to the door. He'd call the FBI if Nikki was in this house.

"Please don't kill her." Nikki's voice. Pleading for Cassie's life.

That was all he needed to hear. Lucas opened the door and walked in.

Elizabeth stood there with a gun pointed at Nikki.

"Elizabeth. What are you doing here?"

Elizabeth looked at Lucas and then at Nikki. Slowly, she moved closer to Cassie.

"She's behind all of this." Nikki sounded more angry than scared.

Two men were lying on the floor. The small hole in the center of each man's forehead confirmed they were quite dead.

"You . . . you did this? Why, Elizabeth?"

"Why? You have to ask me why? All these years, I've waited for you. I took care of you. I helped you. I was more of a wife to you than Victoria ever was. But you stayed with her year after year. I got tired of waiting."

"Victoria?" His mind was numb. What did

301

Victoria have to do with this?

"She died, and you still ignored me. I loved you and you should have loved me. Instead, you went to her." She pointed the gun at Nikki and shot.

Nikki fell to the floor.

His heart thudded with fear.

"Then . . . then I saw her at the hospital." Elizabeth pointed the gun at Cassie. "I knew if you ever saw her, you'd know the truth. I couldn't let that happen. I had to put a stop to it — a stop to them. Or you would never love me."

"Give me the gun, Elizabeth." Lucas's stomach churned as he stepped over a dead body. "It's all over now. Give me the gun."

She stepped closer to Cassie. "No. It's not over until I say it's over." Her voice verged on hysteria. The gun moved away from Cassie and towards him.

Nikki was creeping towards Elizabeth.

Thank You, God. He had to keep Elizabeth focused on him. He moved closer. "You won't shoot me, Elizabeth. You would never hurt me."

"I will. I will shoot you if I have to. I promise I will. Stay back." Her hand shook, but the gun stayed aimed at his heart. Good. Keep her attention away from Nikki and Cassie. He moved sideways towards the door.

Elizabeth turned towards him.

He moved backwards a few more steps.

"I can't let you leave, Lucas. Don't you understand? You've ruined everything. Now you have to pay. It's all your fault. If only you'd loved me."

"I'm sorry. I didn't understand, but now I do. It's not too late for us. We can still be together. Give me the gun. We'll make up a story about what happened to the men. We'll go away together. Nikki and Cassie mean nothing to me."

"I'm not that stupid. I don't believe you."

"You're the one I want."

"You lie. You lie." Her words came out as screams.

Nikki stood up.

Lucas's heart was in his throat.

Blood covered her shirt. She must have been shot. Still, she hadn't given up. She'd keep trying to save Cassie, to save their daughter.

Elizabeth turned towards Nikki and aimed the gun.

Lucas charged forward and grabbed. He wrestled it from Elizabeth's grasp.

"FBI," a voice called from the still-open door.

A moment later, the room filled with FBI agents.

Nikki lay on the hospital bed, irritated at the world. She would not stay here this time.

"Is she OK?" Lucas asked.

"She's fine. Her stitches ripped out. She wasn't shot again."

"I told you so," Nikki snarked. "Can I get up now? I need to go check on my . . . my . . . Cassie."

The doctor nodded. "You can. I'm done with you."

"I'll show you the way." The nurse helped her off the bed. "Your niece is still unconscious, but her doctor said it was from the drugs. They're waiting for them to wear off naturally. Nothing to worry about. Come along. I'll show you where she is."

"Thanks."

Lucas grabbed her hand as they walked to another cubicle.

Nikki didn't resist. She was too exhausted, and besides, it felt good that he'd cared enough to not give up. If he hadn't shown up when he did . . . Nikki shook the negative thoughts away. It was over now. He'd made good on his promise.

Why had she ever thought he wasn't trustworthy?

The nurse took them to ICU. Before she left, she told the nurse in charge who they were. They were asked to sit in the waiting room.

With a gentle voice, Lucas said, "Sit down, Nikki. You look as if you're ready to collapse."

"I don't just look it. I am ready to collapse."

He put an arm around her and helped her to a chair. "You've been through a lot. I called Bethany and Ray. They should be here any moment."

"That's good." Closing her eyes, she put her head on his shoulder.

"It's all over now."

"Almost." She straightened up and stared at him. "Cassie doesn't need to know we are her parents. Ever. It may not have been the right choice back then. But the truth would tear her life apart now." Would he agree? Or would his ego force him to tell her the truth?

Their gazes met.

"I get it. Don't worry. I will never do anything to hurt her — to hurt her family."

Nikki smiled as she nodded. "Good. She's been through enough."

"I promise I'll never say anything to Cassie, ever. You and Mama are right. They are a family and that's the way it will stay. I'll leave it up to you whether you tell Bethany and Ray that I know. But you can assure them I won't ever interfere. But if she needs anything ever, I'll be there to help her."

"I know you will." She put a hand on his arm. "Thank you, Lucas. I know how hard it was to make that choice. You're such a good man. The country will be blessed to have you as a senator."

"I don't know about all that. But I do know that the last thing Cassie needs is another shock. She's been through enough."

"I'm so sorry. I handled everything all wrong. You must hate me for keeping your daughter from you."

He didn't respond.

Her heart broke. She looked over at him.

His smile was so sad. "I don't hate you. You did what you had to do. I understand that, but it still hurts. I won't tell you that it doesn't."

"It gets easier." Enough of this. Time to change the subject. "Did you find out how the FBI found you?"

"When we both disappeared, they figured one of us had been contacted by the kidnappers. The FBI started tracking both our movements, through our phones and Mama's car's GPS system as well. Obviously,

Elizabeth had never called them. I still can't believe she did all this."

"Love can do strange things to people."

"She hurt so many people. I had no idea she was capable of such violence."

"I can't believe I didn't figure it out. It all makes so much sense. She had access to your computers — your phones. It was probably a piece of cake to get remote access to all your gadgets."

"She probably didn't even call a tech guy."

"Or if she did, she simply uninstalled the software she was using and then reinstalled it after he checked it out. Lucas, I just . . . there's no way for you to have known she was behind all this. I hope you won't take the guilt on once again."

"I won't. But I've got plenty of guilt about what you had to go through alone. It must have been so hard for you."

"I made my choices. That's nothing to blame yourself for."

He picked up her hand. "No wonder you freaked out when I walked into your office that day. It's not too late for us, Nikki. We can still —"

"We can't, Lucas. It wouldn't work. We'd always be afraid that Cassie would figure it out. You both have the same beautiful blue eyes. She's a smart girl. We can't take a chance."

"But —"

"My mind's made up. Cassie is more important than —"

"Nikki. Nikki." Bethany ran up with Ray following behind her. "Is Cassie . . . is she OK?"

Nikki rushed over to her sister. "She's fine. They're just waiting for her to wake up from the drugs she was given."

Bethany hugged her. "Oh, thank God. They'd told us that, but I wasn't sure if they were lying."

A doctor walked out from the ICU. "Are Cassie's parents here?"

Lucas and Nikki looked at each other. Then both pointed at Bethany and Ray.

"Great. She's awake, and she wants her mom and dad." He looked at Lucas and her. "Are you family?"

Bethany looped her arm through Nikki's. "This is her aunt. She needs to come in too. She's the one who saved her."

"Actually, that was Lucas."

"All of you go, but only for a few minutes. We'll monitor her for the rest of the night, and if all goes well, she can go home tomorrow."

"I'll be back in a minute," Nikki told Lucas.

He nodded but said nothing.

The doctor led the three of them to a curtained area.

Cassie looked tired but awake.

Bethany rushed to her. "Oh, my baby. My baby."

Cassie smiled. "I'm not a baby, Mom."

"You will always be my baby."

Nikki walked to the other side of Cassie. She bent over and hugged her. "The doctor said I could only stay for a second. I love you and I'm so glad you're OK." Nikki walked away.

She couldn't stay one more moment anyway without saying something she would regret. A part of her wanted so much to tell Cassie the truth. Then she could be with Lucas and have her happily ever after. But that wasn't to be. When she got to the waiting room, it was empty.

Lucas was gone.

25

"Now you're the patient of honor." Nikki tucked the blanket around Cassie. "How are you feeling? Are you warm enough? I can get you another blanket."

"Mom already has three of them on me, Auntie. I'm roasting."

Bethany walked in. "I just got off the phone with Sarah Goode. Apparently, Elizabeth confessed to all of it. Even the murder of Victoria. She'd hired those men to kill Victoria. It's all so . . . horrible . . . such a waste of lives."

Cassie wiped at tears. "Why would someone think killing people was a way to get love? None of it makes sense."

"It's a confusing world we live in." Bethany hugged Cassie. "All the more reason to keep our eyes focused on God. His truth and His wisdom are the only way."

"I can't disagree with that. Don't make all the mistakes I've made," Nikki said.

"You made mistakes, Auntie? That's hard to imagine."

Nikki laughed. "Yeah, right."

Nikki didn't ask why Lucas hadn't called her with the information. As he'd said, he was hurt and angry that she'd kept his daughter from him. She couldn't blame him. Some wrong choices could never be rectified. One only learned to live with the consequences.

She didn't understand why God had let her fall in love with Lucas — again. Just so he could leave her — again. But that wasn't exactly true. She'd never stopped loving Lucas.

God wanted her to make peace with her past and to create a new life for herself. A new future. One where she could be happy.

"I can't believe she had his wife killed," Cassie said. "How awful for him. I never did meet him so I could thank him. For saving us."

"That's OK. I thanked him enough for both of us."

"Still, I would have liked to meet the next senator of North Carolina."

Bethany smiled as Cassie rambled on. When she stopped talking, Bethany said, "Who knows? That still could happen one of these days. Maiden's a small town. What

311

about Kathryn Rites, Nikki? What will happen to her?"

"Charges were dropped. There's nothing illegal about taking a public figure's picture."

She'd told Stanley the same thing. Had his wife forgiven him? Nikki now understood the power of forgiveness. Understood it was the right thing to do. Of course, just as with her and Lucas, forgiveness didn't mean one could erase the past. People still had to live with their choices. And she was willing to live with hers — for Cassie's sake.

"I would love some ice cream, Mom."

Bethany put her hands on her hips. "Are you trying to take advantage of me, young lady?"

Cassie laughed. "Of course."

"Good. You can get away with that for a few more days. And then back to real life."

"I'll get it. Ice cream coming right up." Nikki spoke up. "What flavor do you want? If it's not in the house, I can go to the store."

"Vanilla's fine. It's my favorite."

"Really." She looked at Bethany. "Like mother, like daughter. That's your favorite too."

Their gazes met. Bethany smiled. "Always has been and always will be."

"I find it a bit boring myself, but to each

their own." Nikki grinned. "That's what I say."

Bethany and Cassie laughed.

"You don't know what you're missing, Auntie. Vanilla is the best."

"Whatever," Nikki said as she walked out of the room.

A few minutes later, she walked back in with three dishes of vanilla. Nikki handed one to Bethany and Cassie and then kept the one with hot-fudge sauce for herself.

Everyone dug in.

"I'm leaving today," Nikki announced.

"Today?" Bethany looked up. "You don't have to leave so soon."

"Yeah, I do."

Between bites, Cassie said, "Can't you stay for a few more days?"

"No, I can't."

"But you aren't completely recovered." Bethany looked worried. "Those stitches could come out again."

"I'm recovered enough. I've got things to do."

Bethany's eyes widened. "What kind of things? Please tell me you don't have another case already."

"Nope. You'll both be happy to know there won't be any more cases."

"Why not?" Cassie scooped another bite

of ice cream.

"I'm done with being a private investigator."

Cassie's spoon stopped midway to her mouth. "Why? I thought you loved it."

"I did. But not anymore." She knew in her heart that she wouldn't find the promise of God's peace and joy when she chose to live in a world of too-easy violence. "I'm ready for something new. Not sure what yet, but I know God will open the right doors for me." She grinned at Cassie.

"Good. Getting shot once is more than enough. I don't think I could handle it again. I think you're right to find a new job. And you can move here to do it." Bethany met her gaze full on. "I mean it, Nikki. It's time for you to come home."

Her eyes filled with tears. For years, she'd thought Bethany wanted Nikki to live somewhere else. Away from her — away from Cassie. It was good to know her sister still loved her. "That's sweet, Bethie. And maybe that's what God has in mind, but maybe not. I'll just have to wait and see."

"When are you leaving?"

"In a little bit. Don't worry. I'm a big girl. I can take care of myself."

Cassie laughed. "That's right. She's had hand-to-hand combat training. She's a tough one."

Her sister hugged her. "That may be true but it doesn't stop a big sister from worrying. Now I've got to get these dishes out of here. You know how dirty dishes make me nervous."

After she'd gone, Nikki sat down beside Cassie. "What do you remember about what happened to you?"

"Not a lot." Cassie picked up Nikki's hand. "They will always be my parents."

Nikki turned to Cassie — to her daughter. Their eyes met. She opened her mouth, but nothing came out.

"I wasn't all the way drugged when . . . she was talking. Pieces fell into place. You will always be my very, very special auntie. You did a very good thing making sure I was in a loving family. And God will honor you for that. As will I."

"I . . . I . . ." No words would come.

Cassie squeezed her hand. "It's OK. I always knew there was something very special about you. About our bond. Now I understand. And now you can be with Lucas — if that's what you want."

"Lucas and I don't have a future. Not everything can be fixed."

"I hope it's not because of me."

"Not at all. Too much time and too much

pain." Nikki smiled through her tears. "When will you tell them?"

"Soon — secrets aren't a good thing in a family."

Nikki touched her cheek. "How did you get so wise?"

"I come from a long line of wise women."

"Yes, you do, and your mother" — She indicated the kitchen with a nod of her head — "is the wisest of all."

Cassie smiled at her. "Yes, she is. Mothers are a wonderful thing . . . both of them."

Nikki stood in her office, surrounded by a sea of boxes. She walked over to her computer and stared at the yellow sticky note. It seemed a lifetime ago when Lucas had walked in and all she could see was the word *FORGIVENESS*. She smiled and tore it off the computer. She didn't need the reminder any longer.

The bell above the door tinkled.

"Hey, Robbie. What are you doing here?"

"Are you kidding? I had to come to see the real-life hero for myself. Make sure you were still breathing. You're famous."

"What are you talking about?"

"It's all over the news what happened to you and your niece and that guy running for senator. Must have been some kind of crazy."

"It was. But I can't believe it's on TV." Of course, that made sense. That was too much great publicity to pass up. Even without Elizabeth hounding Lucas.

"So, you got shot, huh?"

She nodded. She raised the arm of her shirt enough to show off the bullet wound.

"And so what? The first time you're shot, you're quitting." He motioned at the boxes.

"I guess I wasn't as tough as I thought I was. It turns out that getting shot hurts." She grinned. "And I didn't like it one bit."

"Can't say I blame you for that. What will you do now?"

"I have no idea. But I can tell you one thing — it won't involve guns or cheating spouses."

"That eliminates a lot." Robbie smiled. "Are you leaving town or staying here?"

"I'm leaving town. Once I get everything packed, I'm having it shipped back to my sister's. Then I'm taking an extended road trip to find myself."

"Still searching for the perfect man, huh?"

She smiled past the pain in her heart. She'd found the perfect man, but it just wasn't meant to be. "Not at all. I told you before I am done with that."

"Too bad." He stepped closer. "I would have liked to have helped you find yourself, Nikki."

"That's sweet, Robbie. But I already told you I'm the weed killer of relationships."

"That's OK. I'm not much of a gardener anyway." He gave her a hug. "Give me a call now and then so I know you're still alive and kicking."

"I'll do that."

He left. Robbie really was a good guy. Why wasn't that enough? She knew the answer. It wouldn't be fair to him or any other man. Her heart belonged to Lucas, now and forever. And even though they would never be together, that fact wasn't going to change.

She turned on the TV that she hadn't packed yet. She surfed until she found one of the news channels. The well-known blonde newswoman smiled. "And this is why that story is even more important, especially for the citizens of North Carolina. Breaking news. This just in."

Lucas flashed on the screen behind a podium. "I'm resigning from the US House of Representatives immediately as well as removing my name from the ballot for US Senate immediately. In light of recent events in my life, I don't feel it would be in the best interests of the good people of North Carolina for me to continue . . ."

She stared, not believing it as he introduced the woman who would finish out his term.

Her door tinkled once again.

She turned.

Lucas stood there.

Her heart flip-flopped. "I . . . I can't believe you resigned and pulled out of the election."

He shrugged and gave her that gorgeous smile. "You said you couldn't be a politician's wife, so . . . I'm not a politician anymore."

Her heart thumped.

She'd been so sure he was hurt and angry. That he never wanted to talk to her again. And yet here he was. He walked closer, his soft blue eyes focused only on her.

Lucas reached out and put his hand in hers.

She wasn't sure if she could breathe.

He knelt down on one knee in front of her. "So, how about it? Will you marry me?"

She stared down at him. "You gave up your life's work for me. I can't let you do that. It was your life's dream."

"No, it was my daddy's dream. Not mine." He grinned. "And besides, you can't stop me. I already did it, but just to clarify, I gave up being a senator for me. I'm tired of politics. Tired of everything I say or do being examined. I don't want to be under that microscope anymore."

"I . . . I don't know what to say."

"Say that you'll marry me. I love you. I want to grow old with you. Sit in a rocking chair on our flower farm and hold hands with you as we watch the sunset. Don't make me ask you again. Oh, well, I'll ask again and again until you give me the right answer. Will you —"

"You don't have to ask again." She knelt down to him and threw her arms around his neck. "Yes, I'll marry you."

" 'Bout time."

Their lips met.

When they separated, she smiled. "Are you sure?"

"I've never been more sure of anything in my life. How about you?"

"I've never been more sure of anything in my life."

They kissed again.

He motioned at the boxes. "What's going on here?"

"I'm quitting the PI business. Did you know it was dangerous? A person could get shot."

"I heard that could happen." He stood up and pulled her up with him. "So, what do we do now that we're both unemployed?"

"Who knows?" Nikki touched his cheek. "We can do anything we want as long as it's what God wants. What do you have in mind?"

"Maybe a flower farm?"

"Maybe, or maybe not. We'll have to think about that one for a while to see who can come up with the best idea."

He leaned in and kissed her again.

This was something she could get used to.

Those soft blue eyes the color of a North Carolina sky twinkled. "Game on!"

The employees of Thorndike Press hope you have enjoyed this Large Print book. All our Thorndike, Wheeler, and Kennebec Large Print titles are designed for easy reading, and all our books are made to last. Other Thorndike Press Large Print books are available at your library, through selected bookstores, or directly from us.

For information about titles, please call:
  (800) 223-1244

or visit our website at:
  gale.com/thorndike

To share your comments, please write:
  Publisher
  Thorndike Press
  10 Water St., Suite 310
  Waterville, ME 04901